$12.95

D1228405

10-06

SHANNON'S EXPRESS

Published by Thomas Bouregy & Co., Inc.
160 Madison Avenue, New York, NY 10016

Library of Congress Cataloging-in-Publication Data

Friend, Charles E.
    Shannon's expess / Charles E. Friend.
        p. cm.
    ISBN 0-8034-9800-4 (acid-free paper)
    1. Shannon, Clay (Fictitious character)—Fiction.
  2. United States marshals—Fiction.   I. Title.

PS3556.R5663S4 2006
813'.54—dc22

                                    2006014218

PRINTED IN THE UNITED STATES OF AMERICA
ON ACID-FREE PAPER
BY HADDON CRAFTSMEN, BLOOMSBURG, PENNSYLVANIA

This story is dedicated to the people of all races, creeds, and national origins whose sweat, blood, and determination drove the railroads westward across America during the latter part of the nineteenth century. Their efforts and their sacrifices joined east and west together, and made the United States, at last, one nation stretching unbroken "from sea to shining sea."

Chapter One
The Train

The train rattled and swayed as it wound slowly through the steep river gorge. In the passenger coach, Clay Shannon wedged himself more firmly into the corner of his seat by the window and resumed his examination of the letter he had taken from his inside coat pocket. The paper was of fine quality, and the gold territorial seal adorning the letterhead seemed far too elegant for the grimy interior of the old railroad car.

"Letter from home?" a high-pitched voice said.

Shannon looked up. The speaker was a short, rotund man sitting in the seat facing him. The fellow was wearing a checkered suit and a battered bowler hat, and the sample case on the seat beside him proclaimed him to be a sales representative of the Sure-Fire Gun Works of Chicago, Illinois.

"No," Shannon said, folding the governor's letter and returning it to his pocket.

"Just wondered," said the salesman. "You looked so

serious I thought it might be bad news." He held out his
hand. "Beamer's the name," he announced, "and selling
guns is my game. Couldn't help noticing that fine looking blue Colt you've got in that tied-down holster of
yours. Those handle grips—ivory, aren't they?"

Shannon ignored the proffered hand.

"Yes," he said, in a tone which he hoped would dis-
courage further conversation.

"Always liked pearl grips, myself," the man went on
enthusiastically. "Got a nice matched pair of our company's pearl-handled .44s in my case here, if you're
interested."

"No thanks," Shannon replied shortly. He did not like
pearl-handled revolvers—pearl tended to be slippery if
the user's hand was sweating—and he did not wish to
engage the fat salesman in conversation. He shifted his
body slightly toward the window and looked out at the
spectacular mountain scenery. The movement caused
his coat to fall away from his side, revealing the badge
on his shirt. The salesman's eyes lit up.

"Ah, a U.S. Marshal!" he exclaimed. "Might have
known that a federal lawman would appreciate fine
weaponry. You headed for Railhead City?"

Since Railhead City was the train's one and only des-
tination, Shannon did not consider it necessary to answer
this question. He continued to stare out the window.

"Quite a place, that," the salesman continued, unde-
terred. "Used to be just a little wide spot on the trail
through the mountains, not much more than a trading
post for hunters and trappers. The railroad's changed
all that, though. Made it into a real boom town. Lots of
action there now—any kind you want, if you know

what I mean. When I was there last month, there were stores and hotels and saloons going up on every corner, and the gamblers and women were flocking in by the dozens. The railroad pays good wages, and when the workers come back into town from the end of the tracks for a little fun, the joint really jumps. I mean, it gets wild. Really *wild.*"

Shannon decided that if he couldn't avoid listening to this imbecile, he might as well get some useful information from him.

"How far beyond the town have they laid the tracks?" he asked.

"Oh, they're no more than fifteen or twenty miles into the canyon yet," the salesman said. "It's slow going in these mountains, you know. And they've had some difficulties, or so I hear."

"What kind of difficulties?" Shannon inquired innocently. The governor's letter had told him exactly what the problems were, but he wanted to hear it from another source, and this loudmouth was obviously ready to oblige.

"Oh, robberies, trouble with the workers, that sort of thing." Beamer glanced around the coach and then leaned forward conspiratorially. "Even sabotage, they say," he confided in a stage whisper.

"And who do *they* say is causing all this trouble?" Shannon asked. The salesman's expression became crafty.

"Ah, now I get it," he said with a wink. "You've been sent to look into all of that, haven't you, Marshal?"

"Perhaps," Shannon said, annoyed at having given himself away.

"Well, I don't like to repeat rumors, you understand," Beamer simpered, "but some folks think that it's . . ."

There was a sudden pounding along the roof of the coach, moving toward the engine.

"What in blazes is that?" Beamer cried.

"Somebody's on top of the coach," Shannon said, listening.

"But why would somebody be running along the roof? You'd have to be crazy to try that when the train's bouncing around like this."

"Maybe," Shannon said. His jaw muscles tightened, for he had a very good idea of the reason for the running footsteps. Unobtrusively, he reached down and slipped the leather thong off the hammer of his six-gun.

Even as he did so, the train lurched violently, throwing the coach's passengers forward in their seats. The squeal of brakes and the screech of metal wheels sliding along steel rails echoed through the car as the train ground to an abrupt halt. The hiss of steam escaping from the engine just forward of the coach and the startled cries of the passengers added to the uproar.

"What in the world is going on?" Beamer squawked, retrieving his sample case from the floor where it had fallen.

Shannon had raised the window by his seat and was attempting to look out, when suddenly the door at the end of the coach burst open and three men wearing bandannas over their faces charged in. The first man was holding a cocked revolver and the other two were carrying shotguns, which they began waving around the coach at the astonished passengers.

"All right, this is a holdup!" barked the man with the

six-gun. "Everybody sit still and don't try nothin' funny, or we'll blow you apart."

"It's a robbery!" Beamer squeaked in terror.

"An excellent deduction," Shannon said drily. He was calmly studying the three intruders, trying to judge their origin, capabilities, and intentions. Their clothing and general appearance suggested they arrived on horseback, and this was confirmed by a quick glance out the window. At the edge of the treeline beside the track, he could see a fourth man hurrying up to the train leading several sweating horses.

One of the robbers produced a burlap bag and started down the aisle with it.

"Come on, everybody put your money and jewelry in the bag," the first gunman bawled. "And I mean *all* of it. Anybody who tries to hold out on us will get a face full of buckshot, and that's a promise."

Shannon could feel a knot forming in the pit of his stomach. From long experience he could see that these gunmen were keyed up to the breaking point, dangerously excited and ready to carry out their threat at the least provocation. They began pushing and shoving the frightened passengers, ripping purses and wallets away from their owners, and stripping watches and jewelry from everyone.

Half-hidden from the gunmen's view by the seatbacks, Shannon slid the Colt out of the holster and held it close beside his leg. He wanted desperately to intervene before someone got seriously hurt, but he knew that if he did there would almost certainly be gunplay, and if that happened the crowded confines of the coach could quickly become a slaughterhouse.

Yet he also guessed that in the end he would have little choice. Angry protests were arising from the passengers now, and Shannon knew that sooner or later someone would try to fight back. All it would take to start a bloodbath would be just one fool who decided to resist.

And one fool did. Just three rows from the front of the coach, a woman screamed and pulled away from the holdup man while he was trying to pluck the rings off her fingers. She flailed at the gunman with her purse, shrieking insults at him. The astounded robber responded by clubbing the woman with the butt of his shotgun, knocking her back into her seat.

"Leave my wife alone!" shouted the man sitting next to her. He leaped to his feet and drew a small pistol from his coat, pointing it at the robber. "Leave her alone, I say!"

The train robber gaped at the enraged husband in disbelief, then raised his shotgun and fired point-blank into the man's body, throwing him violently back against the wall before he crumpled into a heap on the floor between the seats.

"I warned you people!" the outlaw shouted. "Now you're gonna get it!"

Pandemonium broke out as the terrified travelers began scrambling to get out of the line of fire. The situation was out of control, and Shannon could see that the gunmen were about to open fire indiscriminately on the cowering passengers.

Left with no other option, Shannon came out of his seat, his six-gun in his hand. He crouched low in the aisle, trying to see around the panicked passengers, waiting for what seemed an eternity to get a clear view of the outlaws. One of the gunmen saw him and called a warning to his companions, swinging his shotgun toward Shannon as he did so.

"I'm a U.S. Marshal!" Shannon shouted. "Drop your guns!"

He knew that it was a foolish thing to do. By giving the holdup men warning, he made them a present of the time and opportunity to kill him. He should have just opened fire without any preliminaries, yet he owed it to the passengers to try to prevent more bloodshed if he could, and there was a chance—a slim chance, but a chance—that the robbers, surprised to find themselves confronted with an armed lawman, might surrender.

They did not. Roaring obscenities, the first outlaw aimed his revolver at Shannon's heart and fired. The bullet passed through the cloth of Shannon's coat, missing his ribs by a fraction of an inch. Still howling curses, the man began to cock the revolver for another shot.

Shannon squeezed the trigger of the Colt. The heavy .45 bullet struck the train robber in the chest and hurled him back against his two companions. The other two fell cursing in a tangled heap on the floor of the coach, and the second man's shotgun discharged harmlessly into the ceiling. The robber Shannon shot lay still on the floor, but the other two were struggling quickly to their feet. As he rose, the second gunman jammed new shells into the chambers of the shotgun and sent a double load of buckshot down the aisle. The pellets whipped past Shannon, narrowly missing his left ear. Shannon fired again, knocking the shooter over between two sets of seats. The gunman slumped to the floor with his legs, stiff and unmoving, protruding incongruously into the aisle.

Meanwhile the third outlaw was back on his feet, mouthing unintelligible curses and aiming his shotgun at Shannon's head. Desperately, Shannon fired a third time. The man screamed and fell back against one of the seats, his shotgun spinning away over the seatbacks. Moaning, the injured outlaw began crawling on his hands and knees toward the door at the front of the coach.

Shannon started up the aisle toward him to prevent his escape, then saw that the fight was not yet finished. Just as he reached the door, the wounded man rolled over, drew his revolver, and pointed it at Shannon, trying to cock the weapon.

Shannon covered him with the Colt but held his fire.

"Drop the gun!" Shannon called. "It's over. Just drop the gun."

Laboriously, the man dragged the hammer of his six-gun back into the cocked position.

"Don't do it! Don't make me kill you! Just put down the gun! Nobody will hurt you!"

The gunman pulled the trigger. The bullet struck the wooden arm of the seat beside Shannon, driving several small splinters into his arm. Again the wounded outlaw started to cock the six-gun.

Shannon's fourth shot killed him where he lay.

The stunned passengers began peeking hesitantly over the seats at the downed gunmen, looking first at the dead outlaws and then at Shannon as he advanced up the length of the car toward them. Then, finally realizing that the danger was over, the passengers began crowding into the coach aisle, slapping Shannon on the back and shouting congratulations to him.

"Get out of my way," Shannon said, pushing them aside. "I want to get a look at those men."

Quickly he examined the bodies. All of the outlaws were dead.

Mr. Beamer, who had been cowering between the seats during the gunfight, was now close behind Shannon as the marshal bent over the downed gunmen.

"Did you see that, folks?" he trilled. "The marshal's a hero! A *hero*! He got 'em all! He's a hero, I tell you."

"Oh, shut up," Shannon said bitterly. "I wanted them alive. Dead men don't answer questions, and there are a few I'd like to have asked them."

He turned and leaned over the seat to examine the passenger shot by the outlaws. He too was dead. His wife sat beside his sprawled body, sobbing.

"Let me through!" someone yelled. "Let me through, I say. I'm in charge here. What's happened?"

It was the conductor, hurrying toward Shannon from the rear of the car.

"Where have *you* been?" Shannon snapped.

"I was in the caboose with the brakeman. Those owlhoots rode up alongside the train and climbed aboard before we knew what was going on. One of them held us at gunpoint while the others headed up this way. He jumped off when he heard the shots, and I came up here as soon as he was gone. Anybody hurt?"

Shannon gestured at the bodies of the three train robbers.

"These three," he said grimly. "You've also got a dead passenger over there."

"Hey, Marshal, ain't you gonna go after them?" a man called out.

"On foot?" Shannon said, glaring at him. "Be my guest."

He turned back to the conductor.

"Let's get this train rolling again. How long to Railhead City?"

The conductor blinked.

"I dunno—let's see—hour or more, I'd say. Hey, Jonas, what are you doing back here?"

He was speaking to a man dressed in railroad worker's clothing who had come into the coach from the front of the train.

"Is that the engineer?" Shannon asked.

"Naw," said the conductor, "he's the fireman. Jonas, where's Denny? We got to get this train moving."

"Denny's up front in the cab with a busted head," the fireman said. "When they jumped us, he didn't want to stop the train, so they pistol-whipped him."

"Then who did stop the train?" Shannon asked.

"One of them did," the fireman replied with a shudder.

"They knew how to operate the controls?"

"Sure looked like it. They got it stopped, anyway."

"Come on," Shannon said. "Let's see how badly the engineer's hurt."

They found the engineer stretched out on the footplate of the engine cab, conscious but holding his head and groaning. He was bleeding from a cut on his scalp.

"Snap out of it, Denny," the conductor said, propping

the engineer's back against the side of the woodbox. "Can you drive the engine on to Railhead City?"

Denny stared blankly at him and passed out.

"Can somebody else run this thing?" Shannon said to the conductor. "Can you?"

"Yeah," said the conductor, "I done some engine-driving in my time. I guess I can get us there."

"Do it, then," Shannon said. "And while you're at it, you can show me how it's done, just in case somebody shoots you before we hit Railhead City. Now let's get going."

Hesitantly at first, then with gradually increasing assurance, the conductor manipulated the brakes and throttle, and as the fireman shoved wood into the boiler and Shannon watched carefully, the train resumed its journey into the mountains.

Chapter Two
Railhead City

Shannon watched from the engine cab as the train wheezed slowly into Railhead City. The talkative gun salesman had described the place well, for it had all the earmarks of a small settlement grown big almost overnight. Beyond the crude platform serving as a temporary train station, Shannon could make out a sea of tents of all sizes and descriptions, with people in large numbers moving in and out of the open tent flaps. This checkerboard expanse of dirty canvas surrounded several dozen wooden buildings in various stages of construction, some still unpainted but many decorated in garish colors with huge signs proclaiming their nature. Most of the signs said SALOON, but here and there the words HOTEL, BOARDING HOUSE, and CAFÉ could be seen.

Along the hastily nailed-together boardwalks and in the muddy streets, a seemingly endless throng of humanity ebbed to and fro, and a cacophony of tinny music, raucous cries, and an occasional gunshot completed the scene. All of this lay starkly etched against the dark, soaring mountains that rose up behind the town. The crags towered ominously over Railhead City, as if they were watching with disapproval this ugly intrusion into the solitude of the once-peaceful river gorge.

As the still-shaken passengers left the train and scattered through the town, word of the holdup and the shootout spread rapidly, and soon crowds of people were gathering around the train, buzzing with excitement.

Shannon helped the fireman and the conductor lift the still-dazed engineer down from the cab, and then grabbed the conductor by the sleeve as the latter was about to depart.

"Somebody get the sheriff or marshal or whoever's the law in this town," Shannon said.

"Isn't any sheriff," the conductor replied. "No marshal either."

"Is there a doctor?"

"Well, there would have been. He was the passenger who got shot dead on the train."

Shannon sighed in exasperation.

"All right then, is there an undertaker?"

"Oh, yeah," said the conductor. "Well, sort of. The barber takes care of that. Builds the coffins out back of the barbershop. You want me to send for him?"

"No," Shannon said, "I want somebody to haul those dead gunslingers over to his place. Ask the barber to stick them in open coffins and line them up out in front of his shop. I want as many people as possible to get a look at the carcasses. And tell the barber there's a twenty-dollar reward for anybody who can identify them for me."

The conductor hurried away. Shannon pushed his way through the crowd, some of whom insisted upon slapping him admiringly on the shoulder or trying to shake his hand.

A nervous-looking man wearing a rumpled black suit and a deep scowl made his way through the throng.

"Marshal Shannon?" he said, squinting through his steel-rimmed spectacles at the badge on Shannon's shirt.

"Yes?"

"Mr. Morgan wants to see you. Come on, I'll take you to him."

The man turned and started to hurry away.

"Hold it," Shannon said. "Just who are you?"

"I'm Arthur Holloway. I'm chief of security for the railway. Let's go. Mr. Morgan doesn't like to be kept waiting."

Shannon regarded Holloway with a cool eye. Isaac Morgan was the president of the railroad, the man the governor had asked Shannon to come to Railhead City to see.

"Slow down," Shannon said. "I have to get my gear off the train."

"Oh, all right," Holloway said testily, "I'll help you carry it over to the hotel, and then we'll go see Mr. Morgan. But hurry."

The Railhead City Hotel was one of the few wooden buildings that had received a coat of paint, but its newness and sketchy construction were evident. The lobby was sparsely furnished, and the bare floor creaked loudly as Shannon approached the rough counter that served as a desk. The room to which the clerk escorted Shannon was graced by unpainted walls, bare floors, a bed of dubious origin, and a single chair. A small plank washstand was topped by an even smaller washbasin and an empty water pitcher. The burlap curtains that covered the windows had obviously begun life as flour bags.

"Nice," Shannon said, looking around the shabby room. He set his saddlebags at the foot of the bed and placed his rifle scabbard on the rumpled bedcovers while Holloway waited unhappily in the doorway.

"Come on," Holloway said. "Let's go."

"Where is Mr. Morgan now? Is he here in the hotel?"

Holloway snorted in derision.

"Of course not," he said. "He's on his private train, down by the railroad yard. Mr. Morgan travels in style. You'll see."

Shannon did indeed see, as Holloway led him across several sections of track toward a string of cars sitting at the edge of the small railroad yard. In contrast to the dingy appearance of the other rolling stock in the yard, Morgan's private car was a marvel of shining newness. It was a rich maroon color, and on its side the words DENVER & NORTHERN SIERRA R.R. were emblazoned in gold letters.

As Shannon mounted the metal steps and entered the car, he found himself surrounded by sheer luxury. The rear portion of the coach had been turned into a combination of beautifully appointed office and comfortable sitting room. Mahogany paneling covered the walls, velvet curtains were draped over the windows, and the carpeting on the floor was soft and thick. The shades on the

windows had been drawn, and in the light of the gleaming oil lamps which graced the large compartment,
Shannon saw a large, imposing desk at the front of the
room. Behind the desk a man was sitting, watching
expectantly as Shannon and Holloway entered.

Holloway removed his hat and held it nervously in
front of him as he approached the desk.

"This is Marshal Shannon," he said. "I got him here
as soon as I could, Mr. Morgan. I'm sorry it took so
long."

"Come in, Marshal, come in," Morgan said in a deep
baritone voice. "I'm glad you're here. Please take a
chair and make yourself comfortable."

Shannon saw that Morgan was a heavily built man
of middle age, expensively dressed, well-groomed,
and with startlingly bright blue eyes that held
Shannon's steadily. The man did not rise to greet him,
but as Shannon leaned forward to take Morgan's out-
stretched hand, he saw at once the reason for this
apparent discourtesy. Morgan was sitting in a wheelchair with a blanket over his legs, and Shannon
remembered belatedly that the governor had said the
man was partly paralyzed.

Morgan apparently guessed at Shannon's thoughts as
they shook hands.

"Yes, Mr. Shannon," he said, smiling affably. "I'm a
prisoner of this wheelchair. Have been for nearly five
years now, thanks to an outlaw's bullet. Fortunately, I
have a railroad to take me where I want to go. May I
offer you a cigar?"

Shannon declined the offer and settled back into one of
the leather chairs. Holloway hovered in the background.

"Oh, sit down, Arthur," Morgan said. "You look like a schoolgirl waiting for someone to ask you to dance."

Holloway quickly took a seat, squirming uncomfortably on the soft leather.

"Thank you for coming, Marshal Shannon," Morgan said. "I appreciate it very much. I understand you have a letter of introduction for me from the governor?"

Shannon produced the letter from his inside coat pocket and waited patiently while Morgan glanced over it.

"You come well recommended, Marshal," he said. "The governor doesn't bestow compliments lightly, but he seems to think you're the man we need. He says here that you had 'retired' to get married and run a New Mexico cattle ranch. I'm surprised that he was able to pry you away from all that."

"He's an old friend," Shannon said, "and he asked me to help."

Morgan nodded approvingly.

"Loyalty is a fine thing," he said. "It's a quality one doesn't often see these days."

Shannon thought that he detected just a hint of sadness in the words.

Morgan put down the letter on the desk and looked again at Shannon with his keen eyes.

"How much do you know about the trouble we've been having?" he asked.

"Just what the governor told me. It appears that someone doesn't want you to put your railroad through these mountains, and is going to considerable lengths to stop you."

"Exactly. We're working as quickly as we can, trying

to lay track through the river gorge to connect this part of the territory with the rich lands that lie beyond this range. We've got millions of dollars invested in the job already, and hundreds of workers are out at end of track every day laying steel as fast as the terrain and our unseen adversaries will let us. It's slow, hard, back-breaking work, with several fortunes riding on the out-come, and the last thing we need is somebody trying to make things more difficult for us."

He took one of his cigars from its humidor and lit it.

"We need this railroad, Mr. Shannon. And by 'we' I don't mean just me or the other stockholders. The rail-way's important to the people of the entire region. It will build a bridge between this wilderness and the West, bringing us all of the wonders of California and the Pacific coast. It will take us into the twentieth cen-tury if we can put the line through, Mr. Shannon. It will mean trade, prosperity, and, in a few years, statehood."

"Big stakes," Shannon said politely.

"Huge," Morgan said. "Absolutely huge. And it's a gamble we can't afford to lose. The whole territory needs this railroad, needs it badly. And somebody is trying to keep it from happening."

"Exactly what problems have you been having?"

"Just about everything you can think of. Our rolling stock has been sabotaged, our supply trains have been held up—I gather you've seen that for yourself today—and somebody's been trying to run off our work force. Our men have been waylaid in town and beaten up, and two workers have been shot from the mountain slopes by hidden gunmen while they were laying track. A supply shed was burned, and materials

are being pilfered almost every day. The sniping from
the hills is the worst part—the workers are nervous,
and I don't blame them. It's slowed down our progress
considerably, because it's hard to lay track when
you're looking over your shoulder all the time to see if
somebody's about to put a bullet in you. Any more
incidents, and we may have a labor revolt on our
hands."

"What steps have you taken?" Shannon asked, with
a sideways glance at Holloway. Morgan saw the glance
and smiled.

"Arthur here has done the best he can, Marshal. As
you know, he's in charge of security, and he has a force
of railroad police who try to keep things in order.
Regrettably, in the past his people have been concerned
only with the little run-of-the mill matters that any railroad faces—petty theft, unauthorized riders, that sort of
thing. They have no training or experience in dealing
with something this big and well–organized."

Holloway's face was flushed.

"We could have handled it, Isaac," he grumbled.
"You didn't have to call in anybody else. I would have
gotten to the bottom of it in time."

"I know, Arthur," Morgan said soothingly, "but time
is one thing we're short of. It's better this way."

Holloway sat back in his chair, looking as if he had
just been sucking on a lemon.

"You feel that some one person or organization is
doing all of this?" Shannon said, picking up on
Morgan's earlier comment.

"It appears so. I'm not certain, of course, but the
incidents seem to be well-spaced and timed to do the

most harm, and they're evidently instigated by someone who knows quite a bit about railroading."

Shannon remembered that one of the men who
attacked the train that day had known how to stop the
engine.

"Any idea who might be behind it all?"

"Oh, yes. There are a number of people who have, or
think they have, reasons to stop us."

"For example?"

"Indians, for one. The pass through which we'll have
to run track when we reach the top of the river gorge is
considered sacred by a tribe that lives in these mountains. They've got burial grounds up there, smack in the
middle of our projected right of way. I've been negoti-
ating with them to let us come through, but they're not
happy."

"Those three men on the train today were white,"
Shannon pointed out.

"Hunters and trappers have had the free run of these
mountains for decades. They claim the railroad and all
that comes with it will ruin the country, destroying their
livelihood. There are fights between them and our men
here in town all the time. Not likely that they're behind
it—it's too well-orchestrated for that—but there's some
resentment there."

"What about disgruntled workers, men who've been
fired off the job or who have other grudges against the
railroad?"

Morgan shifted his weight in the wheelchair, pausing
before continuing.

"Could be that, certainly. Could even be some of the
big ranchers just east of here. The railroad's already

come to them, taking their cattle to market, and they might want to stop other cattlemen west of the mountains from having the same advantage."

"It sounds as if practically everybody in the territory is a suspect," Shannon said.

"Indeed it does. But there's one particularly obvious candidate."

"And that is . . . ?"

"The St. Louis, Salt Lake, and Western Railway," Morgan replied, shoving his half-smoked cigar into the ashtray on his desk. "Their company is also trying to run a line through these mountains. They're laying track into the range north of here. We're way ahead of them, and they might just be playing foul to give themselves time to catch up."

Shannon nodded. Another railroad competing for the rewards of being first through the mountains would have the motive, the manpower, and the expertise to do the things that Morgan had described. At least it was a starting point, something to go on. If he could determine the source from which the trouble was coming, putting an end to the attacks on Morgan's railway should be relatively simple. But how to begin?

At that moment there was a commotion outside the railroad car. Men were shouting, and a scuffling sound emanated from directly below the compartment in which they were sitting. Then someone cried out in pain, and a voice called out "We got him!"

Holloway remained glued to his chair, eyes wide in consternation.

"Arthur," Morgan said gently, "please go and find out what that's all about."

Holloway blinked, then jumped up and ran from the car.

Shannon regarded Morgan thoughtfully, trying to frame his next comment in a manner that would not offend the railroad man.

"Your Mr. Holloway. How long has he been your, er, chief of security?"

Morgan chuckled.

"Too long, Mr. Shannon. Arthur's my brother-in-law, and for my wife's sake I've given him a job with the railroad. I know he's incompetent, but I've tolerated him up to now because until recently we've had only the usual minor problems that always go along with railroading, and Arthur's lack of ability hasn't been a serious matter. Now, well, now there's too much at stake to leave things in his hands any longer."

"You could just hire more railroad police."

"Yes, I could hire a hundred more drifters and saddle bums, give them clubs, and call them railroad policemen," Morgan said with some bitterness. "But solving this little mystery will require more than brawn and brutality. I need someone with experience, brains, skill, and courage. That's why I asked the governor for help, and that's why he sent me you."

The rear door of the coach opened, and Morgan and Shannon looked up, expecting to see Holloway returning. Instead, another man came striding into the coach, disdainfully brushing dust off the sleeves of his coat.

"Come in, Russell," Morgan said. "I want you to meet Marshal Clay Shannon. He's the lawman I told you about. Marshal Shannon, this is Russell Dalton, vice-president of the railroad and a shareholder in the company."

Shannon took quick stock of Dalton as he shook hands with him. The vice-president was tall, well-dressed, and muscular, as the firmness of his handshake attested.

"Glad to meet you, Shannon," Dalton said. "Isaac's told me quite a lot about you. We're very grateful to the governor for sending you to us. I suppose by now you've heard about our troubles?"

Shannon acknowledged that he had. Dalton's manner was straightforward and friendly, and his eyes held Shannon's without wavering as they spoke. Shannon decided that he had the kind of chiseled good looks that would make him popular with women.

Yet somewhere in Shannon's brain an alarm bell was ringing. Despite the hearty manner and the level gaze, there was something about the man that didn't quite ring true to Shannon. *Perhaps I'm getting too cynical,* Shannon told himself. *I'm starting to imagine that everyone I meet has a guilty conscience.* Yet he could not shake off the feeling that there was something behind those smiling eyes besides welcome. Something faint and fleeting, yet tangible. Could it be . . . fear?

"What was all the racket outside?" Morgan asked.

Dalton shrugged.

"Nothing much. Holloway's numbskulls actually managed to do something right for a change—caught a kid hiding under the car. Indian kid, I think. Looked like he'd been down there for a while. Don't know what he was doing. No sign of any damage to the car. Anyway, they've got him in custody."

"What will they do with him?" Shannon asked.

"I don't know," Dalton said. "Give him a couple of whacks with a billy club and run him off, I suppose. Why?"

"Could your people hold him somewhere until I have a chance to talk with him?"

Morgan and Dalton exchanged glances.

"Certainly," Morgan said. "See to it, will you, Russ?"

"Sure," said Dalton. "Do you want him softened up a little first, Marshal? I can arrange it for you."

"No, no rough stuff, please. Just hold him for me. I'll see him as soon as Mr. Morgan and I are through here."

"Whatever you like, Marshal," Dalton said, grinning. "The governor sent you to save us, and whatever you want, you get. See you later, Isaac."

When Dalton had gone, Morgan looked inquiringly at Shannon.

"Why are you so interested in an Indian boy? I doubt that he was any threat to us. Probably just a petty thief looking for something to carry off."

"Perhaps, but underneath the railroad president's own car seems a strange place for a thief to hide."

"Then why . . . ?"

"It's just possible that he was sent to eavesdrop on our conversation."

Morgan's eyebrows went up.

"You're a suspicious man, Marshal," he said, half-amused.

"Yes, I know. But in my business being suspicious of the right thing at the right time is often what keeps you alive."

Morgan nodded.

"Point taken, Marshal." He glanced at the ornate clock on the wall near his desk. "I see it's getting late, and I'm sure you're weary from your journey, particularly after that incident on the train. Have you taken a room at one of our luxurious local hostelries?"

"Yes, I've already checked in at the Railhead City Hotel."

"There are sleeping compartments on the train. I'm sure we could make you much more comfortable here than you'll be in that roach-trap hotel."

"Thank you, but for the moment I think staying in the hotel will serve our purposes best."

"As you wish, of course. But please plan to have dinner with us here tonight. I want you to meet my family, and we can talk a little more about our difficulties. Seven o'clock suit you?"

"That sounds fine," Shannon said. "Thank you."

"Until seven, then. And let me know what you find out from that Indian boy."

Chapter Three
The Viper's Nest

When Shannon re-entered Morgan's coach at precisely seven o'clock, Isaac Morgan was sitting in one of the deep leather chairs, while Russell Dalton and Arthur Holloway stood nearby. All of them were holding highball glasses, and it was apparent that Holloway and perhaps Dalton as well had already downed more than one drink.

"Good evening, Marshal," Morgan said, waving him to a chair. "The ladies haven't yet made their appearance, so we'll have to wait until they arrive."

He held up his glass, and Shannon heard the tinkle of ice.

"One of the advantages of working in the mountains," Morgan continued. "Ice for the whiskey. Would you care for a drink?"

"Just some cold water, if I may," Shannon said. He had no intention of clouding his head with alcohol on this evening.

"What did you learn from that Indian that was hiding beneath the car?" Morgan asked.

"Nothing, I'm afraid. Your men let him go before I got a chance to speak with him."

Morgan gave Holloway an irritated glance.

"I'm sorry about that, Marshal," Morgan said. "Arthur, your people really must learn to obey orders."

"It could be my fault," Dalton said quickly. "I may not have made it clear to them what they were supposed to do."

"Well, it can't be helped now," Morgan said. "Most likely it wasn't important, anyway."

The forward door of the compartment opened and two women entered. One was dark-haired, in her early forties, Shannon guessed, but still quite attractive. The other was twenty years old at most, blond and dazzlingly beautiful.

Morgan indicated the older woman with a wave of his hand.

"My dear, may I present Marshal Clay Shannon. Marshal, this is my wife, Velda. And this charming child is my daughter, Amy."

Velda Morgan extended her arm with the air of a grand duchess, obviously expecting Shannon to kiss the back of her hand. Shannon touched her hand lightly with his fingertips, then released it and stepped back, nodded to Morgan's daughter, and expressed his pleasure at meeting both of them.

"Shame on you, Isaac," Mrs. Morgan cooed to her husband. "You didn't tell me how handsome Marshal Shannon is. Were you afraid he'd steal me away from you?"

The coyness was not lost on Shannon, nor, apparently, on Morgan himself. Shannon saw the flash of annoyance that flickered across his face as she spoke.

"I'm afraid you're out of luck, there, my dear," he said pointedly. "Marshal Shannon is a married man."

"Indeed?" Velda Morgan said. Shannon could have sworn that she actually looked disappointed.

"Yes," Morgan continued. "To a very fine lady, I'm told. And a very lovely one. The governor tells me that she's the heir of one of the oldest Spanish families in America. They held a large royal land grant in New Mexico and stayed on when New Mexico became part of the United States. Isn't that right, Marshal?"

Shannon nodded curtly. He did not wish to discuss his wife with these people, and especially not with Velda Morgan, for whom he was feeling the first stirrings of distaste.

But he was not to be spared.

"Oh, tell us about her," Morgan's daughter said. "What's her name? And is she really very beautiful?"

"Her name is Charlotte," Shannon said reluctantly, "and yes, she is very beautiful."

"It's too bad she couldn't come with you," murmured Amy Morgan. "We would have loved to have met her, *wouldn't we, Mother*?" This last comment was delivered in a voice that dripped with poison.

"That's very kind of you, Miss Morgan," Shannon said, "but my wife is not able to travel at the moment. She's expecting our first child almost any day now."

"That's splendid, Clay," Isaac Morgan said. "There's nothing like having children, is there my dear?"

"Fortunately not," Velda Morgan said acidly, glaring at Amy.

Astonishing, Shannon thought to himself. *These people all hate each other. What kind of a viper's nest have I gotten into here?*

The uncomfortable silence that followed was interrupted as Morgan's valet and general manservant, a little man named Wimble, entered to announce that dinner was served in the dining car. They trooped in, with Velda Morgan ostentatiously holding onto Shannon's arm and speaking to him in an absurd combination of lordly condescension and syrupy baby talk. Shannon found his dislike of the woman crystalizing rapidly, but he forced himself to respond politely to her comments. Shannon, though no diplomat and certainly no politician, clearly recognized that it was too early to make judgments, and that until he knew more about the situation, it certainly would not be wise to antagonize the wife of Isaac Morgan—or Morgan himself.

The rear half of the dining car was set with a long table down the middle, and around this they took their seats. Shannon was not terribly surprised to find that he had been skillfully maneuvered into a chair between Velda and her daughter, Amy. The mother retained her hold on Shannon's arm even after they had seated themselves, while the daughter regarded him from time to time with sultry looks that were openly inviting.

These women are really giving me the treatment, Shannon thought. *Why?*

But there were no answers yet, so Shannon resigned

himself to his fate. He could see that he was doomed to a long and boring evening, but he nonetheless listened carefully to the conversation, for although he was tired from his journey and the excitement of the day, he knew that he had much to learn and little time to learn it in if he was to carry out the mission on which he had been dispatched.

But the conversation was entirely trivial, and long before they had finished dessert and returned to the sitting room compartment, Shannon had abandoned hope of learning anything of use until he could speak to Morgan again alone.

When they were once more settled in the leather chairs, Amy Morgan leaned forward and smiled sweetly at Shannon.

"Mr. Shannon, I understand that you're a famous gunfighter. I hear you've killed *hundreds* of men."

Shannon's patience was reaching the breaking point.

"I'm afraid you've been misinformed, Miss Morgan," he said tightly. "I'm a lawman, not a gunfighter, and I'm not famous, and I can assure you that I haven't killed hundreds of men."

"He killed three today on that train," said Dalton with a malevolent grin.

"Oh, my," Amy Morgan said breathlessly. "That must *really* have been exciting."

Shannon started to reply, but Isaac Morgan, seeing Shannon's discomfort, intervened. He put down his drink and addressed his wife.

"Well, my dear," he said pointedly, "I'm sure you must be tired. It's been a long day, and Marshal Shannon and I have a little more business to conduct before he returns to the hotel. Would you and Amy excuse us?"

The two women looked sourly at him but rose from their seats to leave. As Velda Morgan turned away from Shannon and her husband and started to lead Amy to the door, her eyes met briefly with Russell Dalton's.

"Good night, Russell," Mrs. Morgan said, extending her hand. "I trust we'll see you tomorrow?"

"Of course, Velda," Dalton said, squeezing the proffered hand.

It seemed to Shannon that the squeeze was just a little too prolonged, and the look that passed between the two just a trifle warmer than it should have been. *Perhaps I was wrong. Perhaps not quite all of them hate each other.*

When the ladies had retired, Morgan again produced the humidor and cigar smoke began to fill the coach.

"Well, Marshal," Morgan said when his cigar was well aglow, "what's the first move?"

"Tell me about this 'end of track,' " Shannon said. "Do you have a camp there?"

"No," Morgan said, shaking his head. "Normally a railroad would have a camp moving from day to day right along with the tracklayers, but in this case we don't."

"Why is that?"

"Two reasons. First, there's no place along the right of way to set up a camp there. You saw on your way up here today how narrow the gorge is below Railhead City. Further up in the mountains, it's even narrower. We're having to blast a roadbed out of solid rock in some places just to get through. No room for a temporary camp, not even room for tents for the workers. The work train hauls one dormitory car for the foreman and some of the key people, but we don't have the rolling stock to bunk all of the laborers on the work train."

"And the second reason?"

"Safety. As I told you this afternoon, we've already had two workers shot by snipers while they were laying track. The men don't want to stay out there at night, where they'd be sitting ducks for some assassin hiding up on the mountain in the dark. So we've started taking our laborers up to end of track on a work train from Railhead City every morning, and the same train brings them back every night."

"I can see how that would slow down your progress considerably," Shannon said. "How far is it? Fifteen miles each way?"

"Nearer twenty," Dalton said. "We lose nearly an hour off each end of the workday, but there's no help for it."

"Tell me about your work force," Shannon said.

"An amazing mixture of backgrounds and nationalities," Morgan said. "Many of them are immigrants— Irish and Chinese mostly, but people from other countries as well. Normally there's not too much friction between the different groups—not while they're on the job, anyway. All are good workers, at least when they're not worrying about being shot at."

"The main difference," Dalton said with a sneer, "is that when they get back here to Railhead City each night, the Chinese go off to their tents quietly, and everybody else heads for the saloons to carouse."

"That's an unfair generalization, Russell, and you

know it," Morgan said reproachfully. "Don't take Mr. Dalton's comment too seriously, Marshal—he has a low opinion of our labor force, I'm afraid. Still, it's true that Railhead City, like most railroad camps, has its diversions—too many of them, in fact. That's another disadvantage of bringing everyone back to town every night. When the men are here, they spend too much time in the saloons and gambling halls. We lose man-hours to barroom fights and hangovers, and sometimes after a big night on the town, some of the men decide that they just don't want to go back to driving spikes the next day, leaving us shorthanded and slowing our progress still further."

"Hangovers or not, one can hardly blame the men for not wanting to go back out on the tracks to work when people are shooting at them from the hills," Shannon said.

"Exactly. So, as you can see, we need your help, Marshal. We need it badly."

He glanced at the clock.

"Well, it's late, Marshal. I imagine that you're ready for some sleep, and so am I. Let's call it a night. What's your pleasure for tomorrow?"

"I'd like to go up to the end of track and look over the situation there. It sounds as if it, and the track in between here and there, are your most vulnerable points."

"Good. If you can be here by five o'clock in the morning, I'll introduce you to my foreman and you can ride up with him on the work train. Go with them, Arthur. Mr. Shannon may have some questions for you."

"Thank you," Shannon said, rising. "Good night, gentlemen. I'll see you tomorrow."

They shook hands all around—Holloway, Shannon noted, with some reluctance—and Shannon moved toward the end of the compartment. He stepped out onto the observation platform at the rear of the car and closed the door behind him. As he started to descend the steps to the roadbed, he realized Amy Morgan was standing in the shadows on the platform.

"Hello again, Marshal. I thought you might like to talk awhile before you went back to that awful hotel." She had changed her clothes since dinner, and the new dress was considerably more revealing than the high-collared one she had been wearing earlier. She was also fanning herself demurely with a little folding fan, which Shannon found odd since there was a distinct chill in the evening mountain air.

"Thank you for your thoughtfulness, Miss Morgan, but I have to be up very early in the morning, and I'd like to get to bed."

"Then perhaps we could walk together as far as your hotel? We could even have a drink in your room, if you'd like."

"Thank you again," Shannon said, a little startled by this rather unsubtle proposal, "but I wouldn't want to leave you to return to the train alone, and in any case, as your father said, it's been a long day."

"Oh, very well," the girl said, pouting. "Perhaps another time."

"Perhaps," Shannon said, stepping off the train and walking rapidly away.

Chapter Four
The Warning

As Shannon crossed the tracks and left the railroad yard, a tall figure materialized out of the shadows and came toward him. Shannon had already drawn the Colt half out of its holster before he recognized the broad shoulders of Russell Dalton.

"Sorry if I startled you," Dalton said. "Mind if I walk with you back to the hotel?"

"This seems to be the night for it," Shannon replied darkly.

Dalton snickered. "Yes, I overheard that little scene you played on the observation platform with the luscious Miss Amy. I'm sorry—I didn't mean to eavesdrop, but I was hoping to have a private word with you before you go up to end of track tomorrow."

"I'm listening."

"Look, Marshal, don't take this the wrong way, because I'm saying it for your own good. I know you've

35

been sent to do a job, but be careful. There are powerful interests involved here. Very powerful interests."

"Mr. Morgan is a powerful man," Shannon said, waiting. He could already guess what was coming.

"I'm not talking about Morgan."

"Who, then?"

"It doesn't matter. Just take my word for it—this is a dangerous situation. It wouldn't pay to be too inquisitive. Somebody could get hurt."

They were passing the open door of a saloon. Shannon stopped in the patch of lamplight that flooded through the door onto the boardwalk and faced Dalton.

"All right, Dalton, what's on your mind? Let's have it straight, no more cat and mouse."

Dalton shrugged. "All I'm trying to say is that it would be better if you tread lightly while you're here. There are certain people involved who won't welcome outside interference in this. And they're willing to be generous. As a U.S. Marshal, you know enough about politics to know that those who cooperate are rewarded."

Shannon stepped forward, grasped Dalton firmly by the lapels, and shoved him hard against the wall of the saloon.

"Take it easy!" Dalton cried.

"And you take this message back to your 'powerful interests,'" Shannon rasped. "This badge isn't for sale. To you or anyone else. I've been sent here to find out what's been going on, and if anybody 'gets hurt' in the process, it isn't going to be me. Have you got all that, Mr. Vice-President? Then get out of my sight."

He left Dalton standing by the wall, staring angrily after him.

"All right, lawman," Dalton whispered. "I warned you."

Shannon locked the door of his hotel room, then took the wooden chair and wedged it securely under the doorknob. He knew the door was so flimsy that a three-year-old could kick it in, chair and all, but long habit had taught him to take whatever precautions he could whenever he could, regardless of how precarious they might be.

He drew the burlap curtains, noting with resignation that they did not quite meet in the center. He was not unduly concerned by this, since only a blind alley and the windowless backs of the buildings opposite lay beyond the window.

The day had been overly eventful, and fatigue was overtaking him. Wearily he removed his gunbelt and hung it on a peg by the door, then removed the six-gun from its holster. Carefully, he cleaned and oiled the Colt, then returned it to the holster and began to prepare for bed. It had cost him a dollar to have the pitcher on the washstand filled with cold water—boomtown prices, he supposed—but he was grateful for the luxury. He poured some water from the pitcher into the basin and washed as well as he could under the circumstances. A towel hung by the washbasin, and he reached out for it.

Just as he touched the towel the window glass splintered inward, the shards knifing through the burlap curtains and bouncing across the wooden floor. The bullet that smashed the window drilled a hole right through the bare boards of the wall opposite it, and in the room next door someone let out a howl of dismay.

The echoes of the gunshot had not yet died away when Shannon reached the window, Colt in hand. Looking through the broken pane, he tried to discern the origin of the shot. He had seen the flash through the opening in the curtains, and knew that whoever fired had done so from just outside the window in the alley behind the hotel. Quickly he raised the broken sash and stepped through. Six-gun in hand, he leaped lightly to the ground and flattened himself against the wall, scanning the darkness of the alley, searching for some sign of movement. The shooter might have run away, but there was a chance that whoever it was had waited in the shadows, hoping to get a second shot. If so, it was a foolish risk, for there was a bright half moon nearly overhead, and there was enough light in the alley to reveal anyone who might be lurking there.

Something moved in the shadows fifty feet down the alley, and Shannon saw someone slipping furtively along the walls, headed for the main street.

"Hold it!" Shannon shouted, raising the six-gun. The moonlight gleamed on the barrel of the Colt as he centered the sights on the moving figure. "Stop right there, or I'll drop you as you run."

The figure whirled into a crouch facing Shannon and fired a second time. The muzzle flash lit the walls of the alley, momentarily blinding Shannon, but he was ready. The Colt barked once, and a loud cry and the sound of a falling body told Shannon that he hit his mark. As the images of the gun flashes faded and his night vision returned, he could see a huddled shape lying near the mouth of the alley. He ran forward, six-gun cocked, and stood over the still form. With the toe of his boot, he rolled the man over on his back, and then, still holding the revolver ready, bent down and lit a match.

The man was dead. Shannon's bullet had struck him in the forehead.

Aimed too high, Shannon thought, as he began to go through the man's pockets. In one of them, he found a large coin, and by the light of a second match he saw that it was a fifty-dollar gold piece. The remainder of the dead man's pockets were empty.

People were coming down the alley now, drawn by the sound of trouble. Someone had an oil lamp which he held over Shannon's head. Shannon saw the lamp-holder was the hotel desk clerk.

"You know this man?" he asked, indicating the corpse.

"Nossir," the clerk said, staring at the body. "Never saw him before. Town's gotten so big, I hardly know anybody anymore."

"Well, he must know somebody that knows me," Shannon said thoughtfully.

He looked up at the gathering crowd.

"All right, folks," he called. "I'm a U.S. Marshal, and everything's under control here. Go on about your business."

He rose to his feet.

"You with the lamp," he said. "What's your name?"

"Maxwell, sir."

"Well, Mr. Maxwell, I'd be obliged if you'd go wake up the barber and tell him that the marshal that came in on the train this morning just brought him some more business."

"Yessir, I'll get him. Here, you want the lamp?"

Shannon took the lamp and stared down at the man he had just killed.

Fifty dollars. There was a time when half a town would have killed me for free. I must be coming up in the world. Or going down in it.

After the barber hauled away the body, Shannon went back into the hotel and placed the borrowed lamp on the desk.

"I'll need another room," he said. "The one I had before is going to be a little drafty tonight."

"Of course, Marshal," the clerk said. "Take number six, just down the hall. Here's the key. I'm sorry about the trouble."

"Not your fault. That room I was in—the bullet went through the wall and into the room next door. I heard someone yell. Was anybody hurt?"

"Nope," the clerk said, chuckling. "Scared the daylights out of the fellow that was in there, though. Some drummer named Beamer, just checked in today. After the shooting he packed up and checked right out again. Swore he was going to sleep on the station platform and catch the first train out tomorrow. Said he was going back to Chicago where the hotels have thicker walls."

Shannon smiled. It was a welcome touch of humor at the end of a very grim day.

But later, as he lay on his bed in his new room, the humor quickly faded, and despite his weariness, sleep refused to come. In the darkened room, images of the day's events kept flashing through his mind, dancing, so it seemed, across the ceiling above the bed, mocking him.

I killed four men today. Four men who were alive this

morning are dead tonight because of me. Of course, they were all killers and they were trying to kill me, and so I suppose they deserved to die, but somehow that doesn't help much. Not now, not here in the darkness.

He began to think of Charlotte, waiting for him at their home in New Mexico. The memory of her gradually replaced the ugly pictures that had been poisoning his mind, and eventually, gradually, gratefully, he faded off to sleep.

Chapter Five
End of Track

The pounding in Shannon's head was getting louder and more insistent. He came awake reluctantly, fighting off the exhausted sleep that had consumed him. The pounding continued, and Shannon realized someone was knocking vigorously on his hotel room door.

"Marshal Shannon!" called a voice from the hallway. "It's me, Maxwell, the desk clerk. It's four o'clock, Marshal. You asked me last night to wake you."

"Thank you, Mr. Maxwell," Shannon croaked. "I'm awake now. Is there any coffee available?"

"Sure thing, Marshal, I'll bring you a cup."

"Make it a whole pot. Hot. And strong, very strong."

He dressed quickly, pausing only to shave. He was bleary-eyed and the mirror over the washstand was dirty and cracked. *It's a miracle I didn't cut my own throat,* Shannon thought, putting away the razor and wiping the last vestiges of soap from his cheeks.

Shannon mounted the steps of Isaac Morgan's coach at a quarter to five. When he entered, Morgan was sitting at his desk, still clad in his nightshirt and examining some papers on the blotter before him.

"Good morning," Shannon said. "I'm a little early. Hope I didn't wake you."

"I wasn't asleep, Mr. Shannon," Morgan replied, shuffling the papers. "I don't sleep much these days anyway. The lead souvenir in my back won't let me. Sounds as if you may have lost some sleep too—I hear someone took a shot at you last night at your hotel. What happened?"

"He missed. I didn't."

There was a firm knock at the door of the compartment. The man who entered at Morgan's invitation was big, burly, and red-faced. His work shirt's sleeves were rolled up above his elbows, revealing his bulging muscles. He greeted Mr. Morgan respectfully and then offered his hand to Shannon.

"Marshal," Morgan said, "this is Pat Kelly, my foreman. He's a rough, tough, hard-drinking Irishman who's as honest as they come and the best foreman who ever ran a railroad. Pat, Marshal Shannon's been sent to help protect your men and get to the bottom of these problems we've been having."

Kelly's grip was like a vise, and his grin was warm and friendly.

"Welcome to the railroad, boyo!" he exclaimed. "Shannon, did you say? An Irish name, surely. Now could it be that your people are from the old country, like meself?"

"My grandfather," Shannon said. Kelly laughed heartily, then turned to Morgan and slapped his hand down vigorously on the latter's desktop.

"Mr. Morgan," he boomed, "You know I don't usually have much use for coppers, but here's one lawman there might be some hope for. We'll make a railroad man out of him, I'm thinking. Now, what can I do for the both of yez this fine morning?"

"I want you to take Marshal Shannon out to end of track on the work train today," Morgan said. "Show him around, let him see anything he wants to see, and tell him anything he wants to know."

"A pleasure," Kelly said, with a heartiness that could only have been genuine.

Arthur Holloway came in, looking disheveled and irritable.

"Well, Arthur," Morgan said with just a hint of reproof in his voice, "glad you could join us. I want you to go up with Kelly and Marshal Shannon on the work train this morning. Stay with the marshal, give him whatever help he needs, and above all keep an eye out for trouble."

"Whatever you say, Isaac," Holloway mumbled. He did not appear to be very happy.

On the next track, a steam whistle began to hoot.

"The work train's leaving," Morgan said. "Good luck, Mr. Shannon. I'll see you this evening. Let me know what you find out."

Riding on the one of the flat cars jammed with workers, Shannon watched with interest as the work train rounded the last bend and end of track came in sight. The train creaked to a stop and stood, the engine venting steam, while the workers disembarked and started up the right of way, past the log barrier that marked the last of the navigable track.

Looking about, Shannon could see why it was impracticable to set up a camp here. On one side of the track the shoulder of the mountain crowded almost to the edge of the roadbed, and on the other side the ground dropped sharply down into the river gorge.

"As we lay the track, we move the barrier forward every day," Kelly explained, as they walked past the engine. "That way we can bring the men and all our tools and supplies right up to the very spot where we stopped work the previous evening."

"How much track are you laying each day?" Shannon asked.

"Bloody little lately. It takes the devil of a time to cut out a roadbed along these canyon walls, and with the workday shortened by the need to haul these lads back to Railhead City every night, we don't get very far very fast. On the open prairie, we could easily lay a mile of track a day—often a lot more. But up here in this gorge, we're lucky if we can put down a hundred yards of steel between sunrise and sunset."

They walked forward until they reached the spot where the track gangs were already hard at work putting down the first rails of the morning. Shannon marveled at the smooth coordination of the effort, as men carried the rails forward with huge iron tongs and lowered them into place, while other workers stepped forward with hammers to spike the rails into the ties. The ringing of steel on steel echoed through the gorge, and the grunts and shouts of the laborers added their own touch to the remarkable scene. With the mountains above them and the rushing white water of the river below, it was, Shannon decided, like some sort of grand industrial ballet performed on a giant and spectacular wilderness stage, a rough job being done by rough men with a degree of skill that made it look deceptively easy.

He noticed also that occasionally one of the workers would glance up apprehensively at the mountainside above them.

"Where was it that the sniper was shooting at your men?" Shannon asked.

"Just back there a bit," Kelly answered, waving a hand back down the track. "The last time was a week ago, and as you can see, we haven't gotten very far since. The boys are nervous, no mistake."

"Holloway," Shannon said, turning to speak to the railroad's security chief, "what have you done about . . ." He stopped, puzzled. Holloway was nowhere in sight.

"Ah, I think the good man's gone on up the right of way a piece," Kelly said. "If I didn't know better, boyo, I'd say from those black looks he's been giving you that he doesn't like you very much."

"I'm not sure that he likes his job very much, either," Shannon said dryly. "He certainly isn't doing much to keep it."

"Ah well, blood is thicker than water, and Isaac Morgan being the kind man that he is, I expect that being the brother of Morgan's wife will keep our friend Arthur employed for a while longer at least."

They walked forward and stood for a moment as

Shannon watched the rails being set into place by the sweating workers.

"Hard work," he said, half to himself. "How's the pay?"

"Good enough," Kelly said. "At least it was until the troubles started. Now . . ."

"Look out!" Shannon cried, shoving Kelly to the ground. High up in the rocks on the hillside above them he had seen a tell-tale puff of white smoke, and even as Shannon pushed Kelly down, the crack of a rifle resounded through the gorge. Clearly audible above the echoes of the shot, the sickening thud of a bullet striking flesh told Shannon that someone near him had been hit. A young laborer who had been driving spikes just a yard away gagged and clawed at his throat, then stumbled off the track and fell to the ground, bleeding profusely. Another puff of smoke appeared, and a second worker went down, screaming in pain as he clutched at his left leg.

The workers were scattering in all directions, tossing their tools aside as they frantically sought cover. Shannon and Kelly had jumped across the tracks and were sheltering behind the rise of the roadbed on the side next to the river. Shannon had his Colt in his hand, and he was studying the rocky wall above them trying to pinpoint the shooter's location. Another bullet ricocheted off the top of a rail just a few feet from his head, leaving a bright mark on the new steel.

"He's got us pinned like butterflies on a card, curse his miserable soul," Kelly muttered.

"Keep everybody down. Tell them to crawl if they have to, but to get back to the cover of the train as quickly as they can."

Shannon tossed aside his hat, checked the cylinder of the Colt, and sprang up.

"Where are you going?" Kelly cried in dismay.

"Up there," Shannon said, starting across the track toward the hill.

"He'll pick you off that rock wall like a fly on a windowpane," Kelly called after him.

"I hope not," Shannon said, flattening himself against the rocks on the uphill side of the track.

The slope was so steep that, pressed against the boulders, Shannon could see little of the terrain above him, but he had formed a reasonably clear picture of the gunman's location. The problem was how to get up there. Carefully, he began picking his way up the slope, moving from one craggy outcropping to another. His boots kept slipping on the stones, and now and then a misstep sent a shower of gravel bouncing down the hillside. Within moments he was gasping for breath, and there were few footholds to aid his ascent. He had to holster the Colt in order to use both hands to raise himself to the next outcropping.

I'm getting too old for this, he told himself as he hauled himself onto the next ledge. The ground was sloping back away from him now, so that it was less precipitous and easier to climb, but the incline also made it hard for him to see what was going on above him. He started upward again, making better progress this time, and finally, after what seemed an eternity, he reached a group of rocks that overlooked the area where he had calculated that the sniper was hiding.

Cautiously, six-gun again in hand, he peered over the

top of the boulders into the little hollow. There was no one there.

He slid down into the depression and looked around. Although the previous occupant of the hollow had vanished, there was ample evidence that he had been there. A half-dozen empty cartridge cases lay scattered on the ground, and a faint odor of gunsmoke still hung in the air.

Shannon holstered the Colt and picked up one of the spent cartridges. A standard .44-40, used by half the rifles in the territory. He held it close to his nose, and noted the acrid odor of freshly burned powder. Examining the shell casing further, he saw a peculiar scratch etched brightly along its brass side. Quickly he collected the remainder of the cartridge cases and checked each one. The scratch was visible on all of them. The rifle that had fired the rounds must have some flaw or burr in the mechanism that was marking the cases as they were inserted or extracted. He pocketed the casings for future reference, and continued his survey of the little hollow. Except for a few disturbed rocks and some indistinct footprints in the gravel, there was no further clue as to the identity of the mysterious rifleman.

Shannon took one last look around, then scrambled back down to the bottom of the hill. He reached the tracks just in time to witness an ugly scene. Several dozen workers were gathered near the front of the locomotive, gesticulating belligerently and turning the air blue with curses. In the center of the ring, Pat Kelly was doing his best to soothe them.

"We ain't comin' out here to be clay pigeons anymore, Kelly!" one worker shouted.

"Yeah, Timmy's dead and Sam's got a slug in his leg. You tell old man Morgan that if he wants any more steel laid on this road, he'd better get us some protection."

"Now, lads," Kelly said in his rich Irish brogue, patting the nearest man on the shoulder. "Sure and I don't like this any better than you do. But you know Mr. Morgan's brought in a federal marshal, and he'll get the lowlifes who are doing this, you can count on it." His tone was conciliatory, but as Shannon approached he could see that Kelly's face was bright red and the veins were protruding along his neck as he fought to control his temper.

"One tin star ain't gonna help," another worker bawled. "We need the Army, that's what we need. I ain't workin' another lick until I know I ain't gonna get my brains blowed out next minute. And you, Kelly, you stop stickin' up for Morgan. He ain't nothin' but a money grubbin' old fool and you ain't nothing but a boot-lickin' company stooge!"

This last was too much for Kelly. The big Irishman drew back one large fist and smashed it into the speaker's face, knocking him flat on his back. A rumble of discontent went up from the onlookers, and a worker standing behind Kelly picked up his heavy sledgehammer and raised it, ready to bring it crashing down on the back of Kelly's head.

"Put down that hammer," Shannon barked, leveling the Colt at the man wielding the sledge. The men in the crowd whirled around, staring at him. For a moment the hammer-wielder froze, the sledge poised in midair. Then, with a curse, he started to swing it at Kelly's skull.

The Colt bucked in Shannon's hand, and gravel flew up between the man's feet.

"Next one goes in your gut," Shannon said, walking up to the man and standing nose to nose with him. "Now put the hammer down and behave yourself before you get hurt."

Cursing, the man reluctantly tossed the hammer to the ground.

"I'll get you for this," he sputtered. "Nobody treats me like that. And anyway, this is between us railroad men. Stay out of it, law dog."

A chorus of agreement went up from the watching crowd.

"Yeah, you better watch it, Shannon," one of them shouted. "We ain't afraid of you or that tin badge you're wearin'. You mess with us, we'll send you home in a box."

"A lot of people seem to want to do that, my friend," Shannon said. "If you want me, you'll have to stand in line."

"Enough of this, you lunatics," Kelly said. "You people are too dumb to know your friends from your enemies, and that's the truth of it."

He turned to Shannon.

"Did you get him?" he asked, jerking his thumb at the mountain.

"No," Shannon said. "Whoever it was had taken off before I could get up there."

"See?" grumbled a worker as he walked away. "I told you that tin star wouldn't do us no good."

"Go on with yez," Kelly roared. "Act like railroad men, not a bunch of snotty–nosed crybabies. Harkness, you and your crew get Timmy and Sam onto the flatcar. We're headed back for town. No more work today."

Footsteps were crunching rapidly along the gravel roadbed toward them. Arthur Holloway pushed through the dispersing crowd and stopped, breathing heavily, in front of Shannon and Kelly.

"I heard shots," he said. "What's the trouble?"

"Bushwhacker," Kelly said, eyeing Holloway with obvious antipathy. "Got two men. One of 'em's dead, and the other won't be driving any spikes for a while."

"Where were you all this time?" Shannon asked, staring keenly at Holloway. The man was sweating profusely, and the knees of his trousers were dirty.

"I went on up ahead to see how the blasting crew were doing. I came back as soon as I heard the gunshots."

"The gunshots were twenty minutes ago," Shannon said. "You must have been a long way up the canyon. A long way."

Holloway's face flushed. "What do you mean by that?" he asked indignantly. "I went up to talk to the blasting crew, like I told you."

"And did you talk with them?"

"Well, no, I hadn't gotten that far when I heard the shots. Look here, Shannon, I don't have to take this sort of thing from you. You've got no reason to accuse me."

"I don't recall accusing you of anything. I just asked you where you were."

"Well, I've told you." Holloway stomped past Shannon and reboarded the train.

Kelly shook his head. "Shannon, me boy, you're making a lot of friends today. A lot of very bad friends.

You think Brother Arthur had anything to do with the shooting?"

"I don't know. He wasn't carrying a rifle when he went up the track a while ago, but it took him too long to get back here after the shots were fired. He was somewhere, and I'll bet it wasn't with the blasters."

"Well," Kelly said, "I wouldn't have thought old Arthur would have the guts to do something like this, but I guess you never know. I'd watch out for him, anyway. He might have just enough sand to put a bullet in your back some fine night. And look out for the big bozo who had the hammer. That's Otto Kurtz, and he's a rough 'un. Strong as an ox and mean as a badger. I saw him break a man's back once in a barroom fight and then put two other men out of work for six months by picking 'em up and heaving 'em through the saloon's front window."

He grinned sheepishly.

"By the by, thanks for stepping in just now. That hammer would have cracked my crown like an eggshell. I owe you one, boyo."

"Come on," Shannon said. "We'd better get that wounded man back to Railhead City."

When the train pulled into the yard in Railhead City, the workers climbed down from the flatcar and began to disperse into town. Many of them cast smoldering looks back at Shannon as they walked away. Shannon, Kelly, and the disgruntled Holloway headed for Morgan's private car.

Morgan was waiting for them. Dalton was present also, pouring himself a drink.

"I heard the work train coming back," Morgan said. "What's wrong?"

Kelly told him.

"I had to bring 'em back, Boss," he said apologetically. "We nearly had a riot on our hands out there. If it hadn't been for Shannon, here, you'd be needin' a new foreman right now, I'm thinkin'."

"You did the right thing, Pat," Morgan said. "Don't worry about it. The man who was hurt—is he being cared for?"

"Yeah, they sent for the barber. He'll patch Sam up all right."

"Go check on him, will you?" Morgan asked. Kelly nodded and left the car.

"The barber seems to be the busiest man in Railhead City," Shannon observed.

"He's the only one in town right now with any medical skills at all. It's ridiculous, isn't it? We brought a company doctor out here when we set up camp, but he quit and went home—said he couldn't stand the place. We had another one on the way up, but as you know he was killed during the robbery attempt on the train."

He turned to Russell Dalton.

"Russ, get a telegram off to company headquarters in Denver. Let them know that the new doctor they sent us was killed, and tell them to get another one up here by the end of the week, no expense spared and no excuses."

"Right away, Chief," Dalton said. He finished his drink in leisurely fashion and then departed without any visible haste.

"Well," Holloway said, "if you don't need me for

anything, I'll go up to the sleeper and change my clothes. Fell down running back to the train," he added, with a sideways glance at Shannon.

When Kelly and Holloway had gone, Morgan looked quizzically at Shannon.

"So, Marshal, any progress?"

"Not much. I've narrowed the suspects down to about a thousand, and I've got at least a hundred theories, none of which seem to fit the known facts. There's one development of interest, though. Here, take a look at this, will you?"

He dug into his pocket and produced the cartridge cases he found on the hill.

"Look at the scratch on the side of the shells. Ever see anything like that before?"

Morgan studied the shell carefully, then handed it back.

"No, sorry. But if you could find the gun that fired these, it certainly would be helpful, wouldn't it?"

"Very. Mr. Morgan, if I'm going to get anywhere with this, I'm going to have to start leaning on some people, and doing some things that other people aren't going to like. Can I count on your support?"

"Absolutely. Do what you have to do, Marshal. I'll back you all the way, no matter whose feathers you ruffle."

"Good. Then I might as well start ruffling. Hello, Holloway. Get all tidied up, did you?"

Holloway had re-entered the compartment, tying his necktie around the collar of a clean shirt.

"What's that supposed to mean?" he demanded.

"Here," Shannon said, holding out the empty cartridge cases. "Take a look at these. Know anybody with a rifle that marks the shell casings like that?"

Holloway picked up one of the shells and looked at it.

"Uh, no, can't say that I do," he said, not meeting Shannon's eyes. "Well, I've got to go. I'll be back in time for dinner, Isaac."

When he left, Morgan looked inquiringly at Shannon.

"Marshal, do you think that Arthur is involved in this?"

"I don't know," Shannon said, "but he was lying about the shell casings. You saw the look on his face— he recognized the mark on them. He may not have fired those shots today himself, but I'm pretty sure he knows who did."

Chapter Six
Chinatown

In the dining car that night, the atmosphere was noticeably subdued. Isaac Morgan seemed preoccupied, Holloway was sullen, Velda Morgan was irritable, and Amy Morgan kept casting resentful looks at Shannon during the meal. Only Dalton seemed cheerful, chatting politely with the unresponsive Velda and flirting with Amy. But Shannon thought he detected a degree of tension beneath the handsome vice-president's smooth patter as well. Could they all be so affected by the shooting incident that morning? *Unlikely,* Shannon decided. *Except for Morgan, not one of these people is the type to lose any sleep over one dead laborer. No, there's something on their minds— every one of them. But what is it?*

The somber meal continued, with Shannon watching unobtrusively for anything that might explain what was going on around him. At one point when Dalton was addressing Amy in a particularly familiar manner,

Velda Morgan glared at the vice-president with obvious displeasure. She looked away immediately, but the annoyance that had flashed across her face was plain enough. *Ho-ho. Motherly protectiveness, or do I detect something more?*

Amy Morgan also gave the appearance of being uncomfortable with Dalton's attentions, and when at one point Dalton leaned over to whisper something to her, she turned and quickly addressed Shannon.

"I understand you went up the mountain trying to catch the person who was shooting at the men today," she said. "That was very brave of you."

"Unfortunately," Shannon said, "the bird had flown before I arrived."

"I also hear that you saved Mr. Kelly from being seriously hurt when that nasty Kurtz fellow attacked him with a sledgehammer," she said. "That was very brave of you as well."

"Not particularly. He only had a hammer. I had a gun."

"Still . . ." Amy said, fluttering her long eyelashes at Shannon.

"How is your wife doing, Mr. Shannon?" Morgan asked. "Have you heard from her?"

"I sent a telegram today, inquiring about her," Shannon replied. He wished these people would stop prying into his private life. Perhaps his irritation was linked to the gnawing worry that he felt for Charlotte, back at their New Mexico ranch waiting for the baby to come. He desperately wanted to be there with her.

"No doubt she's fine," Velda Morgan said with a tart smile that was closer to a smirk. "But you know,

Marshal, you really shouldn't have left her there all *alone,* the poor thing."

Shannon started to point out that if the governor had not called Shannon away to come to the aid of the Morgan family, he would be at home that very moment with Charlotte, but he restrained himself. He did not wish to endanger the success of his mission by clashing openly with Morgan's supercilious wife. It was still too early for that. *But keep it up, Velda, and it's only a matter of time.*

The conversation lagged after that, and it was with relief that Shannon finally excused himself from the table and went back through the train to the observation platform. He wanted some fresh air, some privacy, and some time to think. The air was fresh enough, but he had only a brief period of privacy and little time to think, for he had been standing there looking out at the lights of the town for only a few minutes when Amy Morgan came out onto the platform, wrapping a shawl around her bare shoulders.

"What about that walk, Mr. Shannon? It's a nice night, and there's a moon."

Shannon suppressed a sigh.

"Thank you, Miss Amy, but I have work to do. Perhaps some other time."

Amy Morgan's smile disappeared, and her eyes got hard.

"I can't seem to tempt you at all, Mr. Shannon," she said, her exasperation apparent. "Do you find me so unattractive? Or perhaps you find my mother more attractive, is that it?"

Shannon felt his patience wearing extremely thin.

"You are both quite attractive," he replied, hoping that he was being sufficiently diplomatic, "but I have a job to do here, and I'm afraid that leaves me little time for socializing. I hope you understand. Now, if you'll excuse me, I have to get on into town."

"I'm not used to being ignored, Mr. Shannon," she said archly. "Most men have found me quite pleasing."

"I'm sure they have," said Shannon, starting down the observation platform steps. "Good night, Miss Amy."

"You are very rude, Mr. Shannon," she called after him. "I won't forget it."

Pat Kelly's right, Shannon thought as he reached the ground. *I'm making a lot of friends.*

He crossed the tracks and started down the muddy streets of Railhead City. For some time he walked at random among the maze of tents and hastily-erected wooden buildings, trying to familiarize himself with the layout. He quickly discovered that Railhead City was in reality not one town, but several. The wooden buildings, Shannon noted, tended to be clustered along a single street near the center of the settlement. This semi-permanent sector was surrounded by a broad expanse of tents pitched in untidy clusters, seemingly at random, often crowded in so closely together that there was barely room to walk between them. In some areas, most of the tents housed the sort of commercial enterprises common to all boomtowns, as evidenced by the crude signs painted on the canvas walls or placed outside the tent flaps. In other, quieter locations, sleeping tents predominated, as attested by the darkness of their interiors and the occasional snores audible from within them.

Eventually, Shannon found himself in a section composed entirely of older, often ragged tents, and he quickly realized that this was the portion of town where the Chinese workers had settled. Here there were no bright lights, no tinny pianos, no loud voices. Through the narrow passageways between the tents, figures moved softly in the darkness. There was something almost ghostly in their passage, and although no one looked at Shannon directly, he knew that they had taken careful note of his presence.

As he proceeded through this enclave, Shannon was conscious of a persistent undercurrent of low-pitched sound, a steady hum of voices speaking in Chinese. Occasionally as he passed by a tent he could hear muted strains of music, curious tunes played on instruments unfamiliar to him. From some of the tents drifted wisps of smoke, and Shannon recognized the musky scent of opium. To Shannon there was something unreal about it all, as if he was walking through a foreign land that had magically appeared here in the middle of the familiar western American mountains, and he found it a fascinating experience.

At last he came out of the maze into a sector where the streets were wider and the sights and sounds were more familiar to him. Here the saloons and gambling halls had gathered, and ahead of him one especially large tent, brightly lit from within and with two flaring oil torches flanking the entrance, was emanating the unmistakable clamor of a busy barroom and gambling hall. The sign over the door said EMERALD PALACE and something about the words struck a chord of memory in Shannon's mind.

He pushed his way through the tent flap and found himself in a large room with heavy canvas walls and a wooden floor strewn with sawdust. Along one wall of the big tent ran a plank bar, crude by comparison with many he had seen, but complete with shelves filled with bottles and an ornate mirror behind it. Around the room, faro tables, roulette wheels, and other games of chance were in full sway, and crowds of roughly dressed men were gathered about them. No Chinese workers were in evidence; these men were Westerners, though many of them spoke with accents that were foreign to Shannon's ear. They were shouting, smoking, cursing, and often displaying signs of having imbibed a little too heavily.

As Shannon stood there, taking in the scene, he was startled to see a familiar figure advancing toward him through the crowd. It was Tank Drummond, older but still as elegant as when he had run the finest saloon in Longhorn, Kansas, in the days when Shannon was a young deputy marshal there.

"Hello, Tank," Shannon said with a smile. "I thought the name on the sign seemed familiar."

"Clay Shannon, as I live and breathe!" Drummond said, pumping Shannon's hand. "It's a long time since Longhorn, my friend. Still wearing a badge, I see. That's a surprise—I heard you'd hung up your gun and gone cattle ranching. What in the world are you doing here?"

"I might ask you the same question," Shannon said, glancing around. "Not as fancy as the old Emerald Palace, is it?

Drummond laughed.

"No, but it's just as profitable. When the railroads moved on and the cattle drives stopped coming, all the old Kansas trail towns turned tame overnight. Lots of saloon owners—and lawmen, for that matter—found themselves out of work. So I packed up and looked for greener pastures. The railroad workers are just as thirsty as the cowhands, and the railroad pays better, so now I've got low overhead and lots of well-heeled customers. I miss the old Emerald Palace, but I really can't complain."

Drummond led Shannon to a table in a relatively quiet corner.

"You didn't answer my question, Clay," he said when they were seated. "That's a U.S. Marshal's badge under your coat, so I know you haven't taken up railroading."

Shannon explained his reason for coming to Railhead City.

"Yeah, Morgan's been having a time of it," Drummond said. "You got any idea who's out to get him?"

"No lack of suspects," Shannon replied. "Also no lack of motives and no lack of opportunities. Quite a puzzle, with a strange cast of characters. For instance, I see that Morgan's vice-president is among your customers."

Russell Dalton was indeed standing at the long bar, downing a drink.

"You're right," Drummond said, squinting to see through the tobacco smoke that filled the tent. "Looks a little out of place, doesn't he?"

Shannon nodded agreement. Dalton's expensive suit and well-groomed appearance seemed at odds with the rough atmosphere of the tent-city saloon.

"Not where I'd expect to find him doing his drinking," Shannon said. "Who's that he's talking to?"

The railroad executive was deep in conversation with a younger man whose clothing was considerably less neat and clean than Dalton's. The stranger, who despite the wispy mustache on his upper lip could not have been older than his early twenties, appeared to be agitated, speaking intently to Dalton and emphasizing his words by beating his fist on the bar.

"Don't know him," Drummond said. "Strange pair, I'd say, though. That young fellow looks more like a cowhand than a railroad worker."

"Looks more like a gunfighter than either," Shannon said, noting the two holsters tied low on the younger man's thighs.

Whatever the two were talking about, it clearly was not a pleasant subject, for the young man was becoming angry, and Dalton's replies to him were becoming sharper and sharper.

"Tank, it's good to see you again, and I'd like to stay. But when that character with the twin holsters leaves, I'm going to trail after him for a bit. I'll drop by here again and perhaps we can talk a little more then."

"I understand, Clay. Come in anytime. Watch yourself out there tonight, though. This is a tough town full of tough people, and after dark they both get even tougher. Be especially careful if you go into Chinatown. Don't get me wrong, the Chinese are good people, honest and hard-working. But they keep to themselves when they're not on the job, and they generally don't appreciate strangers who come uninvited into their territory."

"I'll be fine," Shannon said, watching as the conversation at the bar came to a taut conclusion. The young man abruptly turned and stormed toward the door, and Shannon said a quick farewell to the saloon owner and threaded his way through the crowd after him.

He reached the tent's doorway just in time to see the young man untie a paint horse from the hitchrail and lead it off into a narrow passage between the adjoining tents. He was about to follow when Dalton came out of the tent and nearly bumped into him.

"Well, Marshal, nice to see you," said Dalton in a tone that made it clear that he did not consider it nice at all.

"Slumming, Mr. Dalton?" Shannon asked with a bleak smile.

"No, no," Dalton replied, looking away. "I just like to get around a bit, see what the workers are saying about things, keeping my finger on the pulse, as it were."

"Well, don't let me interfere with your duties," said Shannon, still smiling. Dalton started to say something, then changed his mind, bid Shannon a curt good night, and disappeared along the dark street.

Since the young stranger had disappeared, Shannon decided to follow Dalton instead. However, he quickly lost track of him in the darkness and the crowds of workers that were moving through the saloon district.

I'm not doing very well tonight, Shannon thought, disgustedly. *Lost both my pigeons in the space of five minutes. Terrific.*

His attempt to follow Dalton had taken him off the main street and into a maze of tents pitched helter-skelter in an area he had not previously seen. As he cast about for a way back to the street, he heard a commotion to his left. Someone was shouting profanely and Shannon thought he heard a cry of pain. He rounded the corner of one of the tents and found a little clear area. A small crowd of men had gathered, and several of them were holding up lanterns to illuminate the scene. At the center of the circle was a large man who was smashing his fists repeatedly into the face and body of a Chinese worker. The victim was being held erect by two other men holding his arms, and he appeared to be unconscious, or nearly so. In the lamplight, Shannon could see that his eyes were glazed and his face was bruised and swollen. He also saw that the man who was administering the beating was Otto Kurtz, the worker who had tried to crush the railroad foreman's skull that very morning.

Kurtz had drawn his fist back to deliver another blow. Shannon stepped forward and drove the muzzle of his revolver hard into the man's ribs.

"This six-gun's cocked, Otto," Shannon said conversationally, "and it's got a hair-trigger. If you were to hit that man again, I wouldn't be too surprised if you lost a large portion of your liver."

Kurtz whirled to face Shannon, his fist still raised and his face twisted in fury.

"Think about it, Otto. This is one fight you won't win."

Kurtz reluctantly lowered his fist.

"What're you doin' here?" he croaked. "This ain't none of your business."

"On the contrary. When I see a man being beaten

half to death without even a chance to defend himself, it becomes my business. Now what's going on here?"

"This Chinaman knows better than to come around our part of town. I'm teachin' him a lesson."

"School's out," Shannon said. "You two, ease that man to the ground gently and back off. The rest of you, move back too. Go on, do it. I'll shoot the lot of you if I have to."

Grudgingly, the crowd moved back as the two thugs laid the beaten man down on the trampled earth. As they did so, Shannon saw that a Chinese woman was kneeling on the ground a few feet away. Two men were holding her arms twisted behind her. Tears were running down her cheeks and she was staring at the victim's battered face with horror.

"Tell me, Otto," Shannon said mockingly, "were you going to beat her up too? Or might she be too tough for you?"

Kurtz's face was purple with rage.

"You better watch out, Shannon," he said. "We got you outnumbered about ten to one here, and maybe we'll just find out how tough *you* are."

"Excellent," Shannon said. "Let's start now."

He slammed the barrel of the Colt against Kurtz's temple, and the man fell to the ground as if poleaxed. A roar of anger arose from the onlookers, and several of them started forward toward Shannon.

"Come right ahead, boys," Shannon said. "Got six slugs in the cylinder of this Colt that are just looking for a home. Who wants to volunteer?"

Grumbling, the men moved back again.

"Is Otto dead?" someone asked. Before anyone could answer, a groan from the fallen Kurtz answered the question.

"I guess not," Shannon said. "Too bad."

He moved over to the spot where the distraught woman was kneeling on the ground.

"Turn her loose," Shannon said to the men holding the woman's arms. "I won't ask you twice." They released her and stepped back.

Shannon bent over the woman, who was trembling with fear.

"Do you speak English?" he inquired gently.

"Yes," she said, looking beseechingly up at him.

"Do you know this man?" Shannon asked, indicating the beaten victim.

"He is my husband."

"All right, you and I are going to take him home. Give me a hand with him."

Without holstering the Colt, Shannon bent down and pulled the fallen man erect.

"Can you walk?" Shannon asked. The man nodded. "Take his other arm," Shannon said to the woman. "And show me the way."

"This ain't over, Shannon," one of the watching workers said. "Every man in Kurtz's crew will be lookin' for you, and sooner or later we'll catch you when you ain't wearin' that pistol."

"I'll look forward to that," Shannon said. "Meanwhile, pick up your bully boy and haul him back to whatever outhouse he belongs in."

With half-smothered curses and many angry looks at Shannon, the crowd began to disperse. Two of them caught hold of Kurtz's boots and started to drag him away.

With the woman holding her husband's other arm, Shannon began helping the injured man out of the ring of tents and into the darkness.

"Remember what we said, Shannon," someone called. "We'll be seeing you again."

Well, now I've made a few more friends, Shannon thought as they departed. *At this rate, pretty soon I'm going to be the most popular man in town.*

Shannon and the woman laid the injured man on his bedroll in the tiny tent which was their home.

"He needs medical attention," Shannon said. "Is there anyone who can help you?"

"Dr. Lin will help us," the woman said.

"I didn't know there was a doctor in Railhead City."

"He is *our* doctor," the woman replied. "Your people do not consult him."

She smiled wanly.

"Thank you for what you have done for us," she said. "We will remember."

"I'm sorry I didn't get there sooner," Shannon said. "I hope your husband isn't seriously hurt. What about you, are you all right?"

"I will be fine. Perhaps you should go now."

"I understand. But if there's any more trouble, send for me. My name is Shannon. I'm staying at the Railhead City Hotel."

"You are very kind. Good night, Mr. Shannon. And thank you again."

Shannon left the tent and walked slowly back in what

he hoped was the general direction of the hotel. He was sickened by the incident he had just witnessed. A man had almost been killed simply because he was Chinese.

Why is there so much hatred in the world? Shannon wondered, not for the first time. *Why do people hate and kill simply because someone is a different color or practices a different religion or comes from a different country? What's wrong with the human race, that such things happen?* It was a question Shannon had been asking himself all his life, but he knew that there was no answer, and never would be, because there was no reason for these things. None at all. It did not occur to him that it was precisely because such inexplicable tragedies happened that he had chosen, so many years ago, to pin a lawman's star upon his shirt and dedicate his life to fighting against the evils he witnessed— indeed, the very evils that still surrounded him.

He was almost out of the Chinese camp when he passed a particular tent that attracted his attention. The tent was brightly lit inside, and the shadows of two people were visible against the canvas wall, one a man's, the other obviously a woman's. The people were speaking, but though this was still in the Chinese part of town, the voices were not Chinese. Shannon stopped, curious. He could not make out what was being said, but the woman was speaking to the man in very sharp tones. With a start, Shannon realized that the voice was that of Velda Morgan. The man, whoever he was, was responding to her complaints in a manner that was soothing and con-ciliatory. Again, Shannon could not make out the words, but whatever the man had said must have been effective, because the woman's tone soon softened, and a moment later, as Shannon watched, the voices ceased altogether, and the shadows on the tent wall merged into one.

Then the light went out.

Shannon walked slowly back to his hotel, lost in thought.

Chapter Seven
The Enemy Camp

Dawn was just breaking the following morning when Shannon again joined Isaac Morgan in Morgan's office car. Over a cup of steaming coffee, he told Morgan that he had seen Russell Dalton in the Emerald Palace saloon the previous evening. He did not tell him about Velda Morgan or the shadows on the tent wall.

"No, I don't know who that young man might have been who was talking to Russell," Morgan was saying in response to Shannon's question. "You didn't notice the brand on the horse, I suppose."

"No, too dark to see it. Paint horse, though. Almost like an Indian pony."

"Well, it could have been anybody. A town like this attracts all kinds of people, and lots of them. I don't suppose it's important."

"Perhaps not. Does Dalton go into the camp often?"

"Why, yes, he does. He's responsible for keeping all the construction materials moving up the line, and he has to stay in contact with a lot of people to do that. Why?"

"Just wondered. What have you decided to do about the men resuming work?"

"The crews are going back out today," Morgan replied. "It took a lot to convince them, but they finally agreed. I've told Holloway to give his men rifles and put them out flanking the tracks to guard the section gangs. Holloway's people aren't much good, but maybe the sight of the rifles will scare off any more snipers."

"It might, but you're taking a risk putting your crews back out there just now. Is it necessary?"

"I'm afraid so. I don't like it either, but we have to keep working. What are you going to do?"

"So far I haven't had an opportunity to check on that rival railroad company that's trying to beat you across the mountains. Can you show me on your map where they are now?"

Morgan maneuvered his wheelchair over to the large map that hung at one side of the compartment.

"We're *here,*" Morgan said, pointing out Railhead City. "They're running their track right on the other side of the mountain." He pointed to a spot just north of Railhead City, beyond the next peak. "I know from my sources that their camp is now *here.* Are you thinking of going over there?"

"Yes. It looks like it's not too far if I can get over the mountain on horseback."

"That's no problem. There's a low pass *here* and a trail that runs right through it. Some of the traders and trappers use it. It's not always passable in the winter, but this time of year you shouldn't have any trouble. A good horse should have you at the crest in two hours, and another hour or so down the other side ought to put you right in their laps."

"I'll need a good horse, then," Shannon said, wishing momentarily that he had been able to bring his beloved buckskin stallion to Railhead City with him.

"I'll have one here in twenty minutes," Morgan said.

Morgan was as good as his word. He sent a man out to carry the message, and within minutes the owner of Railhead City's livery stable led a spirited bay up to the rear of Morgan's coach and handed the reins to Shannon. Shannon had brought his rifle from the hotel; he slid it into the scabbard and swung into the saddle.

"Food in the saddlebags," Morgan said, "just in case our rivals don't ask you to stay for lunch."

Shannon grinned and set out for the enemy camp.

By late morning he had descended from the low pass and was sitting astride the bay on a little knoll overlooking an encampment that looked like a much smaller version of Railhead City. Although there was movement in the camp, with people going back and forth and a work train puffing slowly away up into the mountains—presumably carrying men and supplies up to this railway's end of track—the level of activity was far lower than that found in the bustling precincts of Railhead City. Clearly the St. Louis, Salt Lake, & Western Railway, despite its pretentious name, was operating on a much smaller budget than was Isaac Morgan's Denver & Northern Sierra.

As Shannon rode into the perimeter of the camp, a man stepped out of one of the tents and leveled a rifle at Shannon.

"That's far enough, mister," the guard said. "Who are you and what do you want?"

Shannon eased back his coat to show the badge.

"I'm Clay Shannon, Deputy United States Marshal. I'm here to see Mr. Allen."

The guard hesitated, then lowered the rifle.

"Okay, Marshal. Sorry. We got to be careful these days."

He led Shannon through the tents to the railroad track. A single siding adjoined the main line, and a lone coach stood on it. It was neither as new or as shiny as Isaac Morgan's private car, but presumably it was better than a tent.

"Wait here," the guard said as Shannon dismounted. "I'll tell Mr. Allen you want to see him."

A few moments later the rear door of the old coach opened, and a tall, a gaunt man came out wearing rumpled gray trousers and a white shirt with the sleeves rolled up. He removed his spectacles as he came down the steps and approached Shannon. His eyes were tired, and he glanced at the badge with something almost like resignation.

"I'm Kenneth Allen," he said, shaking hands. "I guess you must be that marshal that the Denver & Northern Sierra called in a few days ago. Isaac Morgan has influence in the territorial capital, it seems."

"Mr. Allen, let's get one thing straight right away. I was sent to Railhead City, yes, but I don't work for Isaac Morgan any more than I work for you. I was asked by the territorial governor to come to Railhead City to stop the killing and other criminal acts that have been going on there, and to find out who's been trying to sabotage the Denver & Northern Sierra railway. But the badge is neutral, and so am I. If you're having similar troubles, I'll do as much for you."

Allen considered this for a moment.

"Fair enough," he said finally. "I've heard of you, Marshal Shannon. You have a good reputation, and I believe what you say. Come inside, please, and we'll talk."

The interior of Allen's private car was a sharp contrast to the sumptuousness of Isaac Morgan's. It was more spartan, fitted out entirely as an office and cluttered with books and drawings. Some surveying equipment stood in one corner, and piles of papers were everywhere. Allen tossed some books off a chair and waved to Shannon to take a seat. Then he slumped back in another chair and rubbed his eyes.

"Marshal, if you're going to ask me if we've had any troubles like Morgan's been having, the answer is no. We have problems, right enough, but our problems are lack of money, lack of manpower, and lack of time. Nobody's been shot, no rolling stock's been sabotaged. Not yet, anyway."

"It looks like the Denver & Northern Sierra's ahead of you, nevertheless."

"You're dead right there. I've put everything I have into this attempt to cross the mountains ahead of the Denver & Northern Sierra, and we're losing the race. Losing it badly. As you can see, I'm a good twenty miles behind Morgan, and the route we've got surveyed is far inferior to his. We don't have as many men as the Denver & Northern Sierra, for the simple reason that I don't have the money to hire them. And we don't have a good base like Morgan has in Railhead City, so it's tough to maintain the flow of supplies up to end of track. I'm going to keep going as long as I can, but the odds are against me. You can go back and tell Morgan that, if you like. But if you rode over here to ask me if I'm responsible for the shootings and all the other troubles Morgan's had, the answer is no."

"I didn't come to accuse you, Mr. Allen. I'm just trying to get the facts. I see that you know all about what's been happening to the Denver & Northern Sierra. Since it hasn't been happening to you, it appears that it's definitely directed at Mr. Morgan. Can you tell me anything that might help me find out who's doing it and why it's being done?"

"I don't have any answers for you, Marshal. I won't pretend that I'm sorry that he's having trouble, and it's certainly true that anything that slows Morgan down gives me a better chance of beating him through the mountains. But I don't condone killings and I have no idea who's behind them. If I knew anything, I'd tell you. And that's the truth."

He began to cough, burying his face for a moment in a stained pocket handkerchief.

"Sorry, Marshal. They say mountain air is good for the lungs, but it certainly isn't helping mine any."

Noting the cough and Allen's pale face, Shannon couldn't help wondering if Allen was consumptive. Odd, he thought, that Morgan, a cripple, should otherwise be the picture of health, while his opposite number, though not trapped in a wheelchair, looked far less robust.

Allen pulled a watch out of his vest pocket and glanced at it.

"It's nearly the noon hour," he said, "and you must have started out very early this morning. May I offer you some lunch?"

Shannon accepted gratefully, and Allen ordered that food be brought. For nearly an hour as they ate, Shannon remained in Allen's coach, asking questions and trying to size up both the man and the situation. Here was a railroader who had the best motive in the world for trying to sabotage his archrival's progress, a man who stood to gain everything by the Denver & Northern Sierra's troubles and lose everything if Morgan drove first across the mountains and the St. Louis, Salt Lake & Western failed to do so.

Yet somehow Shannon found it difficult to believe that Allen was behind the problems that Morgan was experiencing. Shannon had told someone once that in his profession, it was vital to be a good judge of men and horses. He was judging this man now, and he could not believe that Allen was to blame. And yet the motive was there, a very strong motive, and the two railroad camps were so close together that it would be a simple matter for men in Allen's employ to ride over to the Denver & Northern Sierra's right of way by day or night and do whatever they chose to do to hinder that railroad's progress. Motive and opportunity. But was there the will? Shannon looked deep into Allen's sad eyes and could not find it there.

At length Shannon rose and offered Allen his hand.

"Thank you for your hospitality and your patience in answering my questions," he said. "I'm sorry to have bothered you. If at any time you need my help, send word to Railhead City. I'll come."

"I appreciate that, Marshal," Allen said with a wan

smile. "And please forgive me for doubting your integrity. I guess I'm just jealous of Isaac Morgan's power and connections. He can buy almost anything he wants, but I can see that doesn't include you."

Outside the coach, Shannon retrieved his horse and prepared to mount.

"Just one other question," he said, pausing with one foot in the stirrup. "Do you have any Indians in your workforce here?"

"Why, yes," Allen said, surprised. "We have a few. There are tribes in these hills, you know, and some of their young men appreciate the opportunity to make a little money. We don't use them in the track gangs, but several Indian youths work around the camp doing various jobs. Why do you ask?"

Shannon was thinking of the Indian boy who had been found hiding under Isaac Morgan's private car and had escaped from Holloway's railroad police. He started to ask Allen if he could take a look at any Indians who might be working in the camp that day, then thought better of it. He had not personally seen the boy who had been under Morgan's car, and to make such a request would give away more than it would gain him.

"Thank you again, Mr. Allen," Shannon said, picking up the reins. He started to turn the horse's head when the sound of hoofbeats echoed through the camp and a horseman came galloping full tilt between the tents toward the siding. The rider pulled the horse up hard just in front of the two men and leaped off.

"Who's this?" he demanded, glaring at Shannon.

"Marshal," Allen said, "this is my son, Kenny.

Forgive his bad manners. His mother died many years ago, and I'm afraid that I haven't succeeded in teaching him the social graces."

"Never mind that," Kenny Allen said. "I'll bet this is the tin star that Morgan hired, isn't it? What's he doing snooping around our camp?"

"He came to talk to me," Allen said quietly, "and now he's going back to Railhead City."

"Good riddance, then. Lawman, you leave my father alone. You got no reason to bother us." His youthful face was flushed and his eyes were angry. "You come here again, and you'll have to come through me."

"I'm sorry if I've been a bother," Shannon said mildly. He turned to the elder man. "Again, Mr. Allen, thank you for your hospitality. Good luck."

With a last glance at the son, he turned the bay's head toward the head of the trail and rode out of the camp. At the top of the first rise, however, he reined in and looked back. Father and son were in deep conversation, the father still patient, almost resigned, the younger man animated and obviously angry.

"Interesting," Shannon said. "Very interesting indeed." Kenny Allen, two guns and all, was the young man whom Shannon had seen in the Emerald Palace Saloon in Railhead City the night before, engaged in a similar conversation with Russell Dalton, the vice-president of Isaac Morgan's railroad.

Chapter Eight
The Master

The Emerald Palace was, if possible, even noisier that night than it had been the evening before. Shannon found Tank Drummond presiding over one of the faro tables and chewing on a large unlit cigar.

"See you for a minute, Tank?"

"Sure thing, Clay," Drummond said. He beckoned to another faro dealer who was standing nearby. "Hey Bob! Take over here for a few minutes, will you?"

They retreated to the same corner where they had talked the previous evening. Shannon was stiff and tired from his long ride back from the rival railroad camp, but he needed to talk to Drummond and did not want to postpone it until the following day. He leaned back in the chair, rubbing his leg. As it always did when he rode too long or too far, the old gunshot wound in his knee was bothering him.

"Tank, I went over the pass to the other railroad's camp today. What do you know about Kenneth Allen?"

"Met him a couple of times. Good man, I'd say, but it's plain his ambitions are bigger than his purse. He made a mistake taking on Isaac Morgan, I'm thinking."

"Do you think he could be behind the attacks on the Denver & Northern Sierra?"

Drummond shook his head.

"Doubt it. Allen's got the reputation of being a straight arrow. Honest, knows railroading, treats his men well, lives up to his word."

"Can he beat Morgan to the other side of the mountains?"

"Not much chance, from what I hear. If the rumors are true, he's short of cash, and we know he's already way behind. He'll lose out to Morgan unless the delays Morgan's been experiencing slow the Denver & Northern Sierra down too much. It may not matter to Allen though, because I hear he's dying of TB."

"Know anything about his son Kenny?"

"Never met him, but I've heard talk. He's supposed to be pretty wild, always chasing the girls and getting into fights. A real juvenile delinquent, from the sound of it. Never comes around the Emerald Palace, as far as I know."

"He was here last night."

"He was? Say, you mean he was the youngster talking to Russell Dalton?"

"The same."

Drummond gave a low whistle. "No wonder they made an odd-looking pair. Talk about strange bedfellows. What's the kid like?"

"Fits what you've heard. Typical punk. Too big for his britches, chip on his shoulder, packs two guns because he thinks it makes him look tougher than he really is. More mouth than brains, I'd say. Practically challenged me to a gunfight."

Drummond laughed. "Good thing you were feeling charitable," he said.

"Maybe. That kind talks big to your face and then waits and shoots you in the back."

He leaned forward so that what he was about to say would not be overheard by anyone at the adjoining tables.

"Tank, I need a favor."

"Anything, Clay. You know that."

"I want you to keep an eye out for that kid. If he comes back in here, I want to know when he's here and who he talks to. And if somebody can trail him out of here, or get me over here in time for me to do it myself, it could be a big help. Do you mind getting involved?"

"Not a bit. I'm glad to be able to help. I've got a personal interest, you know. If Morgan goes bust, I'll lose all my paying customers. Then I'll be setting up the next Emerald Palace in one of those Indian villages out in the hills, trading drinks for beads and blankets."

The shout from behind Shannon was exultant.

"Hey, boys, look who's here! It's the great man himself, as big as life."

Shannon turned to find three railroad workers standing a few feet away, watching him. The man in front had his legs spread apart and his hands on his hips, and there was a grin of anticipation on his face. Shannon recognized him as being one of the men who had been involved in the incident with the Chinese couple the previous evening.

"How's your little Chinese girlfriend doing?" the man sneered. "Bet you had some fun with her last night while her old man was out cold."

Shannon sighed. "Go home, little man. You've had too much to drink."

The man, who was a good four inches taller than Shannon's six-foot-two, stepped forward and shook his fist in Shannon's face.

"Come on, law dog," he growled, "hang that fancy gunbelt of yours on the back of that chair and step outside. Let's see how tough you are without your peashooter."

"None of that, Schmidt," Drummond said, signaling to his bouncers. "You know I don't allow trouble in the Emerald Palace."

Shannon stood up. "It's all right, Tank. They'd just wait outside for me anyway. Now, Mr. Schmidt or whatever your name is, how do we do this? One at a time or all three of you at once?"

"Don't worry about that, Shannon," Schmidt gloated. "When I'm through with you, my pals won't have anything left to do, except maybe call your Chinese friends to come pick up the pieces."

"Fine. Let's go."

He bent down, undid his gunbelt, and handed it to Drummond. Then, moving with catlike quickness, he picked up the chair he had been sitting in and brought it down with all his strength on the astonished Schmidt's head. The chair splintered in a dozen pieces and Schmidt collapsed on the floor, whimpering piteously and clutching at his bleeding scalp. The second man started forward, and Shannon drove his fist straight into his red face, sending him tumbling head over heels along the sawdust. He tried to get up, but instead fell back and lay still. Bellowing curses, the third man charged at Shannon. Shannon kicked him hard in the stomach, sending him flying against the wall. He slid slowly to the floor and remained there with his eyes glazed, clutching at his midsection and gasping desperately for breath. The entire fight had taken less than ten seconds.

"Sorry about the chair, Tank," Shannon said, retrieving his gunbelt. He pulled a twenty-dollar gold piece from his pocket and held it out. "This cover the damage?"

"No charge," Drummond said, grinning from ear to ear. "I enjoyed every moment of it. And I don't think you'll have much trouble with these palookas again."

Shannon rebuckled the gunbelt and walked slowly out the door, ignoring the staring eyes of the astounded crowd.

He started back toward the train yard, where he knew that Isaac Morgan would be waiting to hear about his visit to the other railroad's camp. As he neared the edge of the Chinese district, an aged Asian man appeared out of the darkness and stood before him.

"Good evening, honored sir," he said, bowing. "A thousand apologies for interrupting your journey."

"What is it you want?" Shannon said, glancing around to see if anyone else was lurking nearby.

The Chinese bowed again. "The Master wishes to see you, and asks if you could spare him a moment of your so-valuable time."

Shannon looked skeptically at him. Was this some sort of trap?

"Who's the Master?"

"Why, he is the Master, of course," replied the Chinese man with just a hint of surprise in his expression. Then he bowed for a third time. "He begs your indulgence, revered sir, and would be most grateful if you could visit him in his tent."

Shannon's caution was overcome by his curiosity.

"I'll be most interested to meet your Master. By all means, take me to him."

The man bowed once more, then turned and began to wend his way into the maze of tents. Shannon followed, surreptitiously slipping the rawhide thong off the hammer of the Colt as he entered the shadows. His curiosity, though it had overcome his caution, had not entirely eliminated it.

The tent into which Shannon was ushered was large, carpeted, and dimly lit. The light came from candles, not from oil lamps, and there was a heavy scent of incense in the air. At the far end of the tent, an elderly Chinese sat beside a low table. Small brushes, paper, and pots of ink, obviously writing materials, were spread out on the tabletop before him. The man was dressed in robes of patterned silk, and although his hair was grey and his skin was wrinkled with age, his eyes were startlingly bright and piercing as they gazed steadily up at Shannon. As Shannon approached, he arose and bowed politely.

"Good evening, Marshal Shannon. I am Dr. Lin. Welcome to my humble quarters. Will you take a seat?" He gestured at a chair beside the table, and as he did so Shannon noted that his fingernails, though well-kept, were very long, which Shannon recalled having heard was a mark of the Mandarin class—the Chinese aristocracy.

"Thank you, Doctor. Your name was mentioned to me just last evening. I'm very pleased to meet you. I'm Clay Shannon, as you already seem to know."

As he sat down he moved the chair—unobtrusively, he thought—just enough so that he could still see the tent entrance behind him. A faint smile touched Dr. Lin's lips.

"You are safe here, Marshal. No harm will come to you while you are in my presence."

"You're very observant," said Shannon, a little embarrassed. "It's an old habit—moving the chair, I mean. In my line of work it's always best to keep an eye on the door, even if the door is only a tent flap."

"A wise precaution in these perilous times," Lin said with a nod. "Will you have some tea?" he asked courteously, indicating the tea service on the table at his elbow. Shannon had never liked green tea, but he diplomatically accepted the offer, and Dr. Lin gestured to the old man who had led Shannon to the tent. The man, apparently a servant, hastened forward, poured the tea, and presented Shannon with the cup.

"Now, Doctor," said Shannon, taking a sip and then placing the cup carefully on the table before him, "to what do I owe the honor of your invitation?"

Dr. Lin chuckled.

"I see that you share the trait common to most Westerners of, as you put it, 'getting right to the point.' "

"I'm sorry, I didn't mean to be rude, but I'm curious as to why you wanted to see me."

"I simply wanted to thank you for helping my two young friends last night. Your intervention on their behalf was most timely."

"The Chinese couple that were being bullied by that gang of railroaders? I'm glad I could help. I hope the husband isn't seriously injured, and that the wife wasn't too upset by the ordeal."

"They are both recovering nicely, thanks to your courage and your kindness. They are very grateful to you, as am I."

"It's my job to help people in trouble. Besides, anyone would have done the same."

"I fear that few of your countrymen, and certainly very few men in this camp, would have done what you did," said Dr. Lin sadly. "There is some tension between the Westerners and the Chinese community, as you know."

"I know. I'm sorry."

"You have nothing to be sorry for, Mr. Shannon. Your action last night speaks very well for you, and I am indebted to you for it. Therefore, if you will allow me to do so, I would like to try to be of some small assistance to you in return."

Shannon looked sharply at him.

"You're aware of the reason for my being in Railhead City, then?"

"Oh, yes," Dr. Lin said. "Everyone knows why you're here."

"Well, I'd certainly appreciate any help I can get. It's a very puzzling situation."

"And a very dangerous one, Marshal."

"I know. Somebody already took a shot at me

through my hotel room window, and I spent yesterday dodging bullets on the railway."

"I wasn't speaking just of the danger to you, Mr. Shannon, although certainly there is that. But there is danger for others as well, and not just for the poor laborers who have been attacked. Mr. Morgan is in danger as well."

"What sort of danger?"

"Who can say? There are many possibilities."

"Well, then, do you know who is behind all this?"

"Mr. Morgan has many enemies," Lin replied cryptically. "And some of them wish the railroad to fail."

"So I've gathered. What's curious is why so many different people seem to have the same goal."

Dr. Lin's bright eyes looked deep into Shannon's.

"Perhaps, there is more than one goal, and more than one motive."

"An interesting thought. What is your explanation, then?"

Lin folded his arms into the wide sleeves of his jacket and looked down at the table.

"My poor thoughts would be of little use to a man of your experience, I fear. But you will discover the truth, Marshal. I'm sure of it."

Shannon pressed Lin further, but without success. Finally, sensing that the good doctor had said all that he wished to say, Shannon rose, thanked him for his hospitality, and turned to go. As he was about to leave the tent, Lin spoke again.

"Take care, Mr. Shannon. The night is dark, and there are shadows all around you."

Pondering this last remark, Shannon walked swiftly

toward the railroad yard. He felt that Lin's warning had a figurative significance beyond its literal meaning, but nevertheless he kept a careful eye on the shadows through which he passed until he was out of the maze of tents and into moonlight again, crossing the railroad tracks toward Morgan's private train.

Even here a mystery awaited him. As he approached Morgan's coach, he saw someone standing on the observation platform at the rear of the train. As he drew nearer, Shannon realized it was Amy Morgan. She was leaning over the rail of the platform with her back toward Shannon, engaged in whispered but earnest conversation with someone who was standing on the other side of the coach, out of Shannon's range of vision.

"Not so loud," she was saying. "My father's just inside. He'll hear us."

A man replied from the darkness. Shannon couldn't catch the words, but somehow the voice itself was familiar. Then Amy Morgan spoke again, her tone low but urgent.

"You mustn't come here again," she said. "It's too risky. If my father catches us . . ."

"If your father gets in my way," the male voice hissed, "I'll kill him."

"Or he'll kill you," Amy said. "Now go."

"I'll go, but I'll be back later. Wait for me at the same place."

Shannon was now within a few feet of the observation platform. As he reached the tracks, his boots crunched loudly on the stones of the roadbed ballast. Amy Morgan gasped and whirled to face him.

"Who's that?" she cried. "Oh, it's you, Marshal."

"Good evening, Miss Morgan," Shannon said. "I'm sorry if I startled you. Perhaps you'll introduce me to your friend."

"Friend? I don't know what you mean, Mr. Shannon."

The soft sound of footsteps fading into the distance on the other side of the coach told Shannon that there would be no introduction that night to Amy Morgan's friend, whoever he was.

"Amy?" said a voice from within the coach. "Is that you? Is someone out there with you?"

"Why, yes, Daddy," Amy said loudly. "It's Marshal Shannon. That's all."

She gave Shannon a look of utter loathing and disappeared into the coach, leaving the door ajar.

"Come in, Marshal," Morgan called. Bemused by the virulence of the expression on Amy Morgan's face, Shannon walked around the rear of the coach and scanned the darkness beyond, hoping for a glimpse of the man with whom Morgan's daughter had been talking, but no one was to be seen. Shannon ascended the platform steps and entered the car.

He related to Isaac Morgan the events of the day, omitting, however, his meeting with Dr. Lin and Amy's rendezvous on the observation platform with the mysterious stranger.

"It sounds as if you had a long ride for nothing," Morgan said, when Shannon had finished his account of his visit to the camp of the St. Louis, Salt Lake, & Western Railway. "Still, I'm glad to hear that you think Allen's in the clear. Although we've been rivals for years, I've always considered him to be a man of principle, and I find it hard to believe that he would condone sabotage and murder, even for so rich a prize as the one we're pursuing now."

"Nevertheless, someone is after you, and they're playing pretty rough. One more shooting and you'll have a mutiny on your hands. And there's something else too. You won't like it, but we need to talk about it."

"What's that, Marshal?"

"I'm concerned about your personal safety. These people, whoever they are, obviously are willing to kill to get what they want. I'm afraid that you could be their next target."

"Don't be concerned about me, Marshal," Morgan said. He opened the drawer of his desk and withdrew a small nickel-plated revolver. "You see, I have my trusty pistol, and even from this wheelchair I can shoot as well as any man. I'm not worried."

"But I am," Shannon said. "The unpleasant truth is that you're very vulnerable here, Mr. Morgan, confined as you are to this coach in an unguarded railroad yard. Extremely vulnerable in fact. Furthermore, you have your wife and daughter to consider. If you won't think of yourself, think of them. They need more protection than a little .32 caliber pistol kept in a desk drawer."

Morgan frowned, weighing Shannon's words.

"I suppose you're right," he said reluctantly. "In any event, I'll take your advice." He reached over and pulled a bell rope that hung beside his desk. The valet, Wimble, appeared, and Morgan instructed him to send for Arthur Holloway. When Holloway arrived, Morgan said, "Arthur, I want you to pick a dozen of your best men and station them in shifts around the train as guards. I want at least four of them out there at all times, day and night, until further notice. If anyone approaches the train who is not personally known to them, they are to hold the individual outside until I give permission for him—or her—to board."

"All right, Isaac," Holloway said. "I'll put the men on it first thing in the morning."

"I'd prefer tonight," Shannon said. Holloway glowered at him.

"They've gone into town," Holloway said. "I gave them the night off. I won't be able to round them up until tomorrow."

Shannon stared at him, wondering why a man as capable as Isaac Morgan tolerated this fool.

"Well, see to it that they're on duty first thing in the morning," Morgan said.

When Holloway had gone, Morgan turned to Shannon.

"There you are, Mr. Shannon. We'll have guards on duty in the morning. Does that make you feel better?"

"Not really. This is no job for hungover amateurs with billy clubs, Mr. Morgan. Let me wire the governor and ask for some deputy marshals or Pinkerton men to be sent to Canyon City."

"Absolutely not. I appreciate your concern, Marshal, but I won't ask the governor for more help. I don't want word getting around the territory that I'm running scared and need an army to protect me. You're here, and besides, we'll be safe now that we'll have guards posted around the train all the time."

Shannon grimaced. "Yes, you'll have guards," he said, "but even when they're sober, Holloway's men are next to useless—you've said as much yourself. Besides, for all we know, some of them could be in on the plot. For that matter, Holloway might be also."

"Nonsense," Morgan said, amused. "Arthur Holloway is my brother-in-law. Whatever he thinks about me, he wouldn't put his own sister at risk."

"Perhaps, but there's an old Latin phrase that I think applies here."

Morgan laughed. "Quoting Latin, now, Marshal Shannon? I'm impressed."

"I was reading for the law before I became a marshal. Lawyers have to learn many Latin phrases."

"What's the particular phrase you're referring to? And what does it have to do with Holloway or his men?"

"Sed quis custodiet ipsos custodes," Shannon recited somberly. *"But who will guard the guards themselves?'"*

Chapter Nine
Rendezvous

Shannon was desperately tired after the events of the day, but he could not bring himself to go back to the hotel. Instead he waited until everyone on Morgan's private train had retired for the night, and then moved quietly through the darkness across to the next track where the work train sat empty, ready to take the crews up the line in the morning. He entered the caboose coupled to the end of the work train, climbed into the cupola, and wedged himself into the tiny seat from which the train crew watched over the train when it was in motion.

Time and the night crawled by as he sat there. Only the discomfort of his perch and the thousand questions crowding his mind kept him from drifting off into a much-needed sleep.

The moon set just after two A.M.

Soon, now, he told himself. *Stay awake.*

Somewhere there was the faint sound of a door being

discreetly opened and closed. Then, as he watched, he saw a female figure steal out of the sleeping car of Morgan's private train and move hurriedly toward the trees just a few yards beyond the track on the side overlooking the river. The woman had a shawl pulled over her head, but even in the darkness Shannon could see that it was Amy Morgan. She entered the tree line and disappeared down the slope toward the river.

Shannon slipped out of the caboose and started across the open ground, moving as silently as he could. When he reached the tree line he paused, listening for any sound that might give him a clue as to the direction that Amy Morgan had taken after he lost sight of her. The crickets had stopped, disturbed by the intrusion into their nighttime kingdom, but the rushing of the river water a hundred yards below was loud enough to cover any small noise that might have helped him.

Obviously a rendezvous, and probably with the man she was talking to earlier. They must be down this hill, perhaps meeting beside the river. Very romantic.

He started cautiously down the slope, trying to make as little noise as possible. The trees closed in around him, making the darkness complete.

I could walk right over them and never know it. Very inconsiderate of the moon to set just when I needed it. But then, that's what they were waiting for, I suppose.

A dry branch broke beneath the sole of his boot. In the stillness of the forest, the tiny snap seemed to Shannon to be louder than a gunshot. He dropped to one knee, trying to see down the hillside into the blackness. He remained motionless for several minutes, cursing himself for his carelessness, hardly daring to breathe as he strained to hear any telltale sound above the rushing of the water.

Fifty feet to his right, the crack of a rifle ripped through the night. The muzzle flash lit up the trees around Shannon, and a bullet thudded into the trunk of the tree next to his head. Drawing his six-gun, Shannon came to his feet and charged at the spot from which the shot had been fired, crouching low and dodging through the trees. A second bullet fanned past his face, and in the flash he saw the figure of a man rising up from a small thicket just ahead of him, raising the rifle for a third shot. Shannon fired back, but the man dodged as Shannon approached, and Shannon heard his bullet whining off a tree trunk into the darkness. Then he was upon the assailant, leaping over the brush and crashing into the unseen shooter's body, knocking him backwards into the thicket and sending the rifle flying. Shannon scrambled to his feet and lurched forward to grapple with his adversary, but his foot caught on a protruding root, sending him sprawling on his face. He lay there for a moment, half-stunned by the fall, listening in frustration as the noises being made by the fleeing gunman faded away into the trees.

Shannon regained his feet and tried to follow, but he knew that it was too late. Far ahead of him a horse whinnied, and hoofbeats echoed through the trees. Shannon broke out of the tree line just in time to see someone galloping away. Shannon raised the Colt to fire, then thought better of it. The rider might or might not be the same individual who had attacked him in the underbrush, and he did not want to risk killing an innocent person. However, there was one consolation—though it was too dark to identify the departing horseman, there was enough light from the stars and the glow in the sky from nearby Railhead City to see the man's horse as it sped away, and Shannon realized that he had seen the animal before. It was a paint horse, the same one he had seen in the camp of the St. Louis, Salt Lake, & Western Railway the previous day, the paint horse being ridden by Kenneth Allen's son.

Well, well. Curiouser and curiouser.

Amy Morgan came running through the trees. Shannon stepped forward and grasped her arm. She screamed, trying to pull away from him, but he held her firmly in his grasp.

"Calm down, Juliet," Shannon said. "It's Marshal Shannon. You and I are going to have a little talk."

"Let me go! Leave me alone!" She wrenched free and ran headlong back toward the railroad tracks.

Shannon watched her go, then backtracked through the trees to the spot where the ambush had occurred. After casting around through the brush for several moments, he found the rifle that had been dropped by his attacker. He picked it up and headed back up the hill.

Someone aboard the train had heard the shots, for lights were on and several people were outside the cars, calling back and forth excitedly. As Shannon approached Morgan's private coach, Russell Dalton came down the steps, holding a shotgun which he proceeded to point in Shannon's direction.

"Calm down, Dalton," Shannon said. "The fun's over. Let's go inside before the dew rusts that fancy scattergun of yours. I want to see Morgan."

The valet wheeled Isaac Morgan into the car as Shannon and Dalton entered from the rear observation platform. Morgan was in his bathrobe, disheveled but alert.

"What is it, Marshal?" he asked as the valet lit the oil lamps. "What's going on?"

"I think you'd better get your daughter in here, Mr. Morgan. She has some explaining to do."

"My daughter? What's she got to do with this?"

"We'll see. Could you call her in?"

Amy Morgan arrived in the coach a few minutes later, looking both fearful and defiant.

"Why can't you leave me alone?" she said to Shannon.

"I will, as soon as you tell us what you were doing meeting Kenny Allen in the woods at three A.M."

Amy Morgan promptly fainted.

A dose of smelling salts and some sharp questioning by Isaac Morgan produced the story. Amy tearfully admitted she had been seeing Kenneth Allen's son secretly for some time, but she vehemently denied any connection between her liaison with Kenny Allen and the attacks on her father's railroad.

"Please, Daddy, we didn't mean any harm. Kenny's a good boy. He wouldn't hurt anyone. I'm sure it wasn't he who attacked the marshal tonight. It must have been someone else."

Eventually Morgan, obviously shaken by the discovery of his daughter's affair with his rival's son, told her to go to bed.

She turned to go, then stopped and looked at

Shannon. "Back there in the woods, you called me Juliet. Why?"

"Your little rendezvous with the son of your father's enemy reminded me of the story of Romeo and Juliet."

"Who are they?" Amy asked, frowning.

"Never mind," Shannon said. "It's not important."

Amy Morgan gave him a look of sheer hatred and flounced out of the compartment.

When she had gone, Isaac Morgan rubbed his eyes wearily and looked at Shannon. The pain on his face was all too evident.

"Do you think that it was Allen's son who tried to kill you in the woods?" he asked.

"I think it's likely, but I have no proof. I didn't get a look at the shooter's face. It's possible that it could have been someone else, someone who followed me into the trees. Or who followed your daughter or Allen, for that matter."

He picked up the rifle he recovered from the underbrush and held it close to one of the oil lamps. Carefully directing the muzzle away from the others in the compartment, he worked the lever that opened the breech of the rifle. A spent cartridge case popped out and rolled across the rug. Shannon retrieved it and held it under the lamp.

There was a bright scratch down the length of the casing.

Shannon reached into his pocket and pulled out one of the empty shell cases he found on the mountain above the tracks the day the workmen were shot. He compared the two carefully, then handed both shells to Morgan.

"The scratches are exactly the same," Morgan said, raising his eyes to meet Shannon's.

"Yes," Shannon said. "Exactly the same."

Dawn was breaking when Shannon finally returned to the hotel and stretched out, fully clothed, on the bed. Despite his exhaustion, sleep was slow in coming. After the exertions of the past twenty-four hours, the old wound in his leg was making itself felt very plainly, and the pain, combined with the hard mattress and the thoughts racing through his brain, effectively defeated slumber.

So Morgan's daughter and Allen's son were carrying on an affair despite the rivalry between their fathers. But was there in fact a connection between the Allens and the attacks on Morgan's railroad? Amy had described the younger Allen as a "good boy," but nothing Shannon had seen of young Allen, from his mistreatment of his horse to the two guns strapped low on his thighs, fit that description. And although it was now certain that Kenny Allen was the late night visitor Amy Morgan met by the river, was it Allen who shot at Shannon farther up the slope?

I've probably got enough to arrest him, but I'd never make it stick in court. It's always the same—what I know and what I can prove are two different things.

He turned restlessly on the lumpy bed, filled with a growing frustration. Half clues, coincidences, too many suspects, too many motives, too many questions, too few answers. And he needed answers soon, before anyone else got hurt. But what to do? And how to do it?

As the first rays of morning penetrated the half-closed burlap curtains, he finally fell asleep.

Once again it was a loud knocking on the door that roused Shannon.

"Who is it?" he called, trying to gather his thoughts.

"It's me, Mr. Shannon. Maxwell, the desk clerk."

"What do you want?"

"I've got a message for you. It's from Mr. Drummond at the Emerald Palace Saloon."

Shannon groaned and sat upright on the bed. He felt as if he'd hardly closed his eyes.

"What time is it?" he asked.

"Nearly noon."

Shannon staggered to the door, still half-asleep, and took the small piece of paper that Maxwell handed him.

He's here.

"Coffee, Maxwell," Shannon said. "Three cups this time."

Shannon dressed hurriedly, downing the steaming coffee as he did so. Then, somewhat revived, he hurried through the settlement toward the Emerald Palace. He had no doubt about the meaning of Drummond's message. He had asked the saloon owner to let him know if Kenny Allen returned, and so, it seemed, he had.

Although it was only noon, sounds of revelry could be heard from within the Emerald Palace as Shannon drew near. As he approached the door, he was not surprised to see Allen's paint horse tied up at the hitch rail. The animal looked tired, and there were fresh rowel marks on its sides. Shannon walked around to the paint's right side and looked at the saddle scabbard. It was empty.

As he entered the tent, Shannon swept his eyes over the room. Kenny Allen was sitting at a table in the far corner, a bottle in front of him and a very bored and weary-looking saloon girl sitting beside him.

Tank Drummond saw Shannon come in, and hurried over.

"He came in early this morning," Drummond said, smothering a yawn. "My people didn't tell me about it until a few minutes ago. I generally stay up pretty late, watching the place, so I was still asleep when somebody finally called me. Sorry it took so long to get the message to you."

"That's all right. I was sleeping late myself. Thanks for letting me know."

"Be careful with him," Drummond said, jerking his thumb in Allen's direction. "He's been hitting that bottle pretty hard, and he's in an ugly mood."

"So am I," Shannon growled.

Allen looked up belligerently as Shannon approached. It seemed to Shannon that Allen's face paled slightly when he recognized the marshal.

"What the devil do *you* want?" Allen said, reaching for the bottle.

Shannon picked Allen up by his shirt front and pulled him erect, then drove his fist hard into Allen's face. Allen went backwards over the table and crashed to the floor. He lay in the dirty sawdust for a moment, stunned by the unexpected blow, then sat up, still dazed.

"What'd you do that for?" he whined.

"Unfinished business from last night. Get up."

Allen struggled to his feet, his surprise turning to wrath as mopped his cut lip with his neckerchief.

"I'll get you for this," he said, staring in disbelief at the bloodstains on the neckerchief. Shannon righted the overturned chair and shoved Allen into it.

"Shut up, Junior. I want some answers from you."

"I don't know nothing about last night. I just got to town this morning."

"Skip the nonsense. Amy Morgan's spilled the beans. However, if you're nice and helpful to me, I might just be able to keep Isaac Morgan from having you strung up from the nearest tree."

Allen blinked. His face was now definitely paler.

"I didn't do nothing with Amy. We just talked."

"Sure you did. But I don't care about your little romance with her. Your saddle scabbard's empty. Where's that rifle I saw in it yesterday?"

"I dunno," Allen said, looking away. "I guess some-body stole it."

"Or maybe you lost it in the woods last night. Right after you tried to shoot me with it."

"You got nothing on me," Allen said sullenly. His surprise was rapidly turning to anger. He stood up and his hand dropped to his holster.

"No two-bit law dog is gonna treat me like this. You better get away from me or I'll blow your head off."

His bloodshot eyes were wild now, and Shannon

could see the rage boiling up in him. Shannon stepped back a pace and faced him.

"All right, I'll give you your chance. Let's see how fast you are with those two big, bad pistols of yours." He slipped the thong off the hammer of the Colt. "Go ahead. Make your play."

Allen hesitated, his right hand now nearly touching the handle of one of his revolvers.

Tank Drummond stepped between them, putting his hand on Allen's arm.

"Don't try it, kid," he said. "I've seen Shannon draw. If you touch that gun, he'll kill you where you stand."

Allen froze, and Shannon saw first indecision, then fear in his eyes.

"I ain't drawing on no U.S. Marshal," he said, moving his hand away from his holster.

"Don't let the badge stop you," Shannon said. He reached up with his left hand and unpinned the metal shield from his shirt, tucking it in his pocket. "Now it's just between the two of us. Well?"

Allen sat down and reached for the bottle.

"I ain't fighting," he mumbled.

Shannon kicked the chair out from under him and again hauled him to his feet. Holding Allen by the back of his shirt and the seat of his pants, he propelled the startled young man to the door of the saloon and shoved him out onto the boardwalk beyond. Allen caught the hitchrail to prevent himself from falling and looked back at Shannon, fury mixing with the dread in his eyes.

"My father—"

"Yes, let's talk about your father. Does he know

you've been shooting unarmed men from ambush? If not, I just can't wait to tell him. I'll bet he'll be really proud of you when he hears about it."

Allen's face was now dead white.

"I ain't shot nobody," he squealed. "I don't know what you're talking about."

"We'll see. I've got a rifle that I'm keeping as evidence. If and when somebody identifies it as being yours, I'll be coming for you. Tell your father that. Oh, yes, and one other thing you'd better know."

"Yeah?" Allen growled, untying his reins from the hitchrail and mounting the paint horse. "What's that?"

"If I ever—and I mean *ever*—see another bloody mark on that horse's side, I'll take those sharp-pointed spurs of yours and shove them right down your lying throat—straps, rowels, and all. Now get out of this town, you little hoodlum, and don't come back."

Allen hesitated, and for a moment Shannon thought he was going to go for his gun. Then he cursed, wheeled his horse, and galloped away. Shannon noted with satisfaction that he did not use his spurs in the process.

"Good grief, Clay," Drummond said, coming out of the saloon and standing beside Shannon as Allen rode off. "You haven't mellowed any in your old age, have you?"

"Lack of sleep always makes me grouchy. Speaking of which, do you happen to have any coffee in that gin mill of yours?"

Drummond brought two mugs of hot coffee to the table where Shannon was waiting and sat down opposite him.

"Pretty early for the place to be this crowded, isn't it?" Shannon asked, looking around at the busy room.

"We never close. But, yes, it's busier than usual today. The railroad crews didn't go to work this morning. They refused to do anything more until Morgan finds some way to protect them."

"I'd better get over to the yard, then. Morgan may need some backup. First, though, I appreciate the benefit of your local knowledge. Who is this man called Dr. Lin?"

"Have you met him?" Drummond asked.

"Yes, he invited me to his tent last night."

"You've been honored, then. The Chinese call him the Master. He's the closest thing we've got to an MD in this town, and from what I've seen, he's a better physician than any Western sawbones I've run across this side of the Mississippi."

"This is a strange place to find a man who seems so learned. What's he doing in Railhead City?"

"I don't know. Nobody knows, at least nobody but the Chinese, and they aren't talking. He just appeared one day after the Chinese community was established. But I can tell you this—the Chinese workers worship him. He has tremendous power among them, and if you want something in this town, don't go to Morgan. Go to Lin."

Shannon put down his coffee cup.

"Thanks, Tank. I'd better get back to the train. I've got a feeling things must be pretty tense there right now."

Shannon found Morgan at his desk, looking very solemn.

"I hear the men wouldn't go to work today," Shannon said, sinking into one of the leather chairs. "What about tomorrow?"

"They agreed to go, finally. I had to offer them double pay and a bonus, and I promised them you'd start coming up to end of track with them, to keep an eye on things. That all right with you?"

"Fine."

"Thank you," Morgan replied, looking relieved. "In that case I recommend that you move your gear over here from the hotel this evening. We've got a compartment in the sleeping car that you can have. You can spend the night and then ride up on the work train with the laborers in the morning."

"Sounds good. I see that Holloway's got his people guarding the coaches now."

"Yes, for whatever that's worth."

"Then I'll go back to the hotel and bring my things over here, as you suggest. It's getting late, and I don't want to be coming back here after sundown. One of Holloway's merry men might decide to shoot me in the dark."

He returned to the train within the hour and was ushered by Morgan's manservant, Wimble, to a compartment in the sleeping car. It was not as elegant as Morgan's coach, but it was clean, well-appointed, and infinitely more comfortable than the hotel.

"I hope this will be satisfactory, sir," Wimble said, opening a door at one side of the compartment. "As you see, you have a small private sanitary facility in here. Meals are served in the dining car, but if you'd prefer to eat here in the compartment, just let me know and I'll be happy to bring you your food."

"No, thanks," Shannon said. "I wouldn't miss this evening's family gathering for the world."

Wimble departed, closing the door softly behind him. Shannon raised the curtain on the window and looked out. The sun was just setting, and its fading light filled the compartment. Shannon turned away from the window again, and felt a strange chill run along his spine as he saw that the sun's dying rays pouring through the window glass had temporarily painted the compartment's walls blood red.

Chapter Ten
The Shadows

Dinner was a sullen affair. The conversation was desultory and for the most part nonexistent. Isaac Morgan seemed preoccupied. Amy Morgan picked at her food and threw occasional hostile looks at Shannon. Before they were midway through the meal, Shannon found himself wishing that he had accepted the valet's offer to serve dinner to him in his own compartment.

Just as dessert was being served, there was a knock on the door, and the foreman, Pat Kelly, entered, hat in hand, looking unhappy.

"What is it, Pat?" Morgan asked.

"Mr. Morgan, we've just discovered that some dynamite is missing from the explosives shed."

"Dynamite?" Morgan put down his spoon. "How much?"

"Two cases. Just flat gone. The blasting crew went to get their supply for tomorrow, and found the lock on the door busted."

Shannon's stomach tightened.

"Anybody see anyone going in or out?" he asked.

"If they did, they ain't telling," Kelly said. "I questioned everyone that might have been near the place today. No dice."

"That settles it," Morgan said. "I'm taking this train up to end of track tomorrow, and we'll keep it there for the next few days. If there's going to be more trouble, I want to be there when it happens. Clay, you can ride up with Russell, Arthur, and me on this train instead of taking the work train as we planned."

"Do we have to go too?" his wife asked unhappily.

"No, my dear. You and Amy can stay here in the hotel if you like."

Velda Morgan made a sour face.

"Not in that horrible hotel," she said. "I'd rather stay on the train. It's just that there's nothing to *do* up there in the mountains."

"I'll stay here," Amy said decisively. "I *loathe* end of track."

"I don't want you in Railhead City alone," Morgan said, equally decisively. "If your mother's going up with the train, I'd prefer that you did too. You can keep her company while we're there."

"Oh, *Daddy,*" Amy said petulantly. She threw her napkin down on the table and rose to leave the car.

She had barely risen from the table when there was a sound of breaking glass outside the dining car, and a burst of flame leaped up the outer wall of the car, completely obscuring one of the windows.

Shannon was on his feet immediately.

"Everybody out!" he shouted. "Amy, get your mother off the train. Dalton, you and Wimble and the cook help Mr. Morgan. Get everybody around to the side of the train away from the fire. Holloway, come with me."

Shannon leaped down the dining car steps and raced back to the flames that were licking up the side of the car. As he approached, he saw the pieces of broken glass lying along the track, and smelled the oily odor of kerosene.

"Firebomb," he said. "Holloway, where are your men? They're supposed to be on guard out here."

As he spoke, two railroad security men rushed up carrying buckets of water, which they proceeded to slosh on the flames.

"We just went to get something to eat," one of them said apologetically.

"There's supposed to be four of you," Shannon snapped.

"Yeah, Joe and Turk are coming with more water."

Several other people, attracted by the commotion and the fire, were now running up with buckets. Within seconds the flames had been extinguished, leaving only a black stain on the side of the wooden car and the lingering smell of smoke and kerosene.

"We saw him," one of the guards said. "He threw the bottle at the train and then ran."

"Just one man? What did he look like?"

"Dunno," said the guard. "Didn't get a very good look at him in the dark."

"Did anybody go after him?" Shannon demanded.

"Well, no. We figured we'd better get the fire out first."

"Brilliant," Shannon said. "All right, which way did he go?"

"Down there. Past the first row of tents at the edge of the yard."

Shannon drew his six-gun and ran in the indicated direction. Plunging between the tents, he hunted about for several minutes, hoping to catch a glimpse of the bomb-thrower. As he rounded the corner of one tent, someone leaped up from the shadows ahead of him, fired a single shot in his direction, and then fled into the darkness. Shannon went after him, dodging tent ropes and other obstacles half-seen in the dark. The fugitive was headed for the center of town, and in a moment Shannon came out of the maze of tents onto the street where the larger saloons and gambling halls were. There were men moving up and down the street, but no one was running or acting in a suspicious manner.

Disgustedly, Shannon holstered the Colt and looked around. The Emerald Palace was just a few steps away, so he went in.

Tank Drummond was at the bar, talking with one of the track gang foremen. When Shannon entered, Drummond came over to him.

"You're getting to be a regular customer, Clay. What's up?"

Shannon told him about the firebombing of the train. Drummond gave a low whistle.

"Sounds like somebody's raising the stakes," he said.

"If so," Shannon replied, "it was a pretty feeble effort. We got the fire out before it did much damage, and nobody was hurt."

"Still, it sounds as if they've upped the ante a bit. Any idea who it was?"

"No. Anybody come in here within the last few minutes breathing hard?"

"Not that I noticed. But people come in and out all the time. Say, I hear that Morgan may take his private coach up to end of track tomorrow. Is that true?"

"Yes, it is. How did you find out about it so fast?"

"He apparently told some of his people earlier today that he was thinking about it. Didn't know he'd decided to do it."

"Well, he has," Shannon said gloomily, "and I'll bet everybody in this town knows it before midnight."

He took his leave of Drummond and started back to the railroad. To save time, he left the main street and cut through the tents, pondering the night's events as he walked. As he had told Drummond, the firebomb attack on the dining car had been a weak effort at best. The bomb-thrower must have known that a small fire like that would be put out quickly, before any significant damage had been done. It was almost as if it was just intended to frighten them all, rather than doing any real harm. But what was the point? Were the perpetrators hoping to scare Morgan into abandoning the attempt to drive the railroad through the pass? Hardly credible that anyone would seriously believe that Morgan would do that over so small an incident. Then what was the purpose of the attack?

And then there was the business about the missing explosives. Was it just another harassing petty theft, or was there some more sinister purpose? And if so, what?

And now the news about Morgan taking the train up to the end of the line the following day was spreading through the camp. Everyone would know about it, including the people who were trying to stop the railroad's progress. What did it all mean?

A theory was forming in his mind when he was distracted from his thoughts by a peculiar feeling that was stealing over him. He found himself with the strange but distinct impression that someone was following him. There was no reason for this sudden apprehension, for he had seen no one trailing him. He whirled around and studied the area behind him, but no one was in sight.

Perhaps I'm imagining things. This affair is making me paranoid.

He continued on, but he could not shake off the feeling that he was not alone. Now on high alert, he increased his pace, trying to reach the railroad yard and escape the unseen watchers that were dogging his steps.

Abruptly, several men materialized out of the darkness ahead of him. The moon was still up, and there was enough light spilling out of the surrounding tents to enable Shannon to see that it was a group of railroad workers. They formed a line in front of him, blocking his path. Some were carrying hammers, others had crowbars or other tools. The man standing in the middle of the line had a double-barreled shotgun, and it was aimed right at Shannon's midsection. Shannon saw that the man holding it was Otto Kurtz, and he recognized some of the others as part of the gang that had attacked the Chinese couple the night before.

"Okay, Shannon," Kurtz rasped. "We're tired of you beating up our people. Now we're going to make you pay."

Shannon tensed, ready to draw the Colt. With a shotgun in the hands of the brutish Otto Kurtz pointed at his abdomen, he knew that he was in serious danger of not living to see the morning.

"Don't go for that smokepole," Kurtz warned, cocking the hammers of the shotgun. "I got you covered dead cold with this smoothbore. You try to drag out that pistol, and I'll cut you in half. So stand still and take your beating like a man, law dog. Get him, boys!"

The men moved forward, hefting their weapons. Shannon was still debating whether to draw and risk the shotgun, when his adversaries stopped suddenly, staring past Shannon at something behind him in the semi-darkness. Shannon turned, and saw that a dozen Chinese laborers had silently appeared in back of him. They were armed with long knives and strange looking hatchets that they were holding at the ready.

At first Shannon thought that he was trapped between two groups of assailants, but then one of the Chinese stepped forward and spoke loudly to Kurtz and the other men blocking Shannon's path.

"You will please to leave quietly," the Chinese man said. "Mr. Shannon is under our protection."

"Oh, yeah?" Kurtz retorted. "What makes you think you people can take us on? We'll crack your heads for you, that's what we'll do."

"Look behind you, Mr. Kurtz," the Chinese spokesman said calmly.

Kurtz looked, and so did Shannon. A solid wall of Chinese workers had materialized behind Kurtz's rabble. Kurtz and his men now found themselves suddenly facing odds of at least four to one.

"Well, Otto," Shannon said, drawing the Colt. "It

seems you've picked the wrong night for your little party. Those axes they're carrying look pretty efficient. If I were you, I'd do like the man says and take a walk."

"I can still get you with this shotgun," Kurtz said. His voice was not quite as firm as it had been when he first confronted Shannon.

"Maybe," said Shannon, "but I'll get you first— remember that. No matter what happens to me, you won't live to enjoy it. Now make your choice. Fight or run, it's all the same to me."

Kurtz stared at him for a moment, then looked about him at the solid ring of armed Chinese workers that surrounded his little group. Slowly he uncocked the hammers of the shotgun and lowered the muzzle.

"There'll be another time, Shannon," he said. "Your Chinese pals won't always be around to help you."

"You'd better hope there isn't another time," Shannon said. "I've taken all I'm going to take from you. Next time I'll kill you on sight. *On sight,* Kurtz. No talk, no questions, no warnings. I'll just shoot you down in the mud and leave you to rot there. Understand? Good. Then get out of here before I decide to do it now instead of later."

The Chinese stepped aside to let Kurtz's gang through. Shannon watched them go, then turned to thank his benefactors. But there was no one there. As silently as they had come, they had vanished into the night.

"Good evening, Mr. Shannon," said a quiet voice at his elbow. "A fine night, is it not?"

Shannon whirled, startled. Dr. Lin was standing beside him.

"Well, Doctor, it appears that I'm in *your* debt now. Thank you."

"A small favor," Lin replied. "I'm glad that we could return your earlier kindness. Good night, Marshal."

And then he too was gone.

Shannon started again for the railroad yard. As he holstered the Colt, he was annoyed to note that his hands were shaking slightly. *Must be the cold. Getting chilly. Should have worn a warmer coat.*

He left the shadows, grateful to see once more the lights of Morgan's train ahead of him.

"It's not good enough, Mr. Morgan," Shannon said. "Holloway's people are worthless. You need better protection, and tonight proves it. Say the word, and I can have a dozen deputy marshals here this time tomorrow."

"The answer's still no, Clay. If we did that, everyone in the territory would say I was running scared. I can't afford that. This is railroad matter, and I want to keep it that way."

"Very well, let railroad men take care of it, but we need better railroad men than Holloway's got."

"What are you suggesting?"

"Send for Pat Kelly, would you?"

Kelly was there in short order.

"Mr. Kelly," Shannon said, "you know what happened tonight. We need some better people to guard Mr. Morgan and his family. If Mr. Morgan approves it, could you get together some good men to act as guards for this train? We need long-time railroaders, men with no grudge against Mr. Morgan, men you can absolutely trust. Can you do it?"

Kelly didn't hesitate.

"How many do you want?" he asked with a grin.

"I'd say twelve. Three shifts of four men each. It would mean pulling them off other work, but we have no choice now."

"I'll get you two dozen, if you need them," Kelly said. "And I'll get you some of my good Irish lads, men who would gladly guard all night and work all day if it would help Mr. Morgan, here. When do you want them to start?"

"Tonight, if possible. Two patrolling each side of the train, around the clock. Nobody gets aboard unless Mr. Morgan or I give them the green light."

"On my way!" Kelly said, and departed.

"We'll be pulling out at five A.M.," Morgan said, "so that we can be laying track by dawn. We've got some ground to make up. You're settled aboard the train?"

"Yes," Shannon said, "but I won't be traveling up with you on the train tomorrow."

The theory that he had been forming when Kurtz's gang interrupted him was now firmly in his mind.

"I don't understand. The men are counting on you to be there."

"I'll be there," Shannon reassured him. "I just have to take care of something else first. I'll ride up on horseback during the day. You can tell the men I'll be there by mid-afternoon at the latest."

"That's a pretty long ride," Morgan observed doubtfully.

"Not as long as the trip over the mountain to visit your rivals the other day. Which reminds me, may I have the use of that big bay stallion again? He's strong and knows how to keep his footing in the rocks."

"Of course. I'll have him brought over first thing in the morning."

"Oh, well, no need to have anyone bring him over," said Shannon carelessly. "I'll pick him at the livery stable when I want him."

Outside the coach, angry voices could be heard arguing back and forth. Presently the door of the compartment burst open and Arthur Holloway came charging in, his face red with anger.

"Isaac, why have my men been replaced?" he demanded indignantly. "Kelly's out there posting some of his work crew as guards. He's told my people to leave."

"That was done on my advice," Shannon said. "Sorry."

"Your advice? Why?"

"Nothing personal. We just decided that your people are better suited to other duties."

"You mean you don't trust them!" Holloway cried. His face was twisted with anger and embarrassment as he turned to Morgan.

"Isaac," he said, "I'm sick of being humiliated like this. I'm chief of security for this railroad. First you call in this . . . this outsider here, and then you replace my men with a bunch of tracklayers."

"I felt it was for the best, Arthur," Morgan said. "Please trust my judgment."

"But I'm your brother-in-law," said Holloway plaintively.

"Yes, Arthur, you are."

Holloway uttered an expletive, then turned on his

heel and stormed out of the coach, slamming the door behind him.

"Poor Arthur," Morgan said. "But he'll get over it."

"I hope so," said Shannon, weighing in his mind the degree of Holloway's ire and the possible consequences of it. Was it enough to make Holloway a threat to Morgan?

Isaac Morgan was studying Shannon keenly, a half-smile on his face.

"I don't know what you have in mind for tomorrow, Clay, but I can see you're up to something. Whatever it is, be careful. You seem to have a lot of people angry at you right now."

"I've certainly made a host of friends here. Unfortunately, most of them hate my guts."

Chapter Eleven
Ride into Danger

Fearing that word might get around of his real intentions, Shannon had deliberately left Morgan and the others with the impression that he was going to do an errand in Railhead City the next morning and then ride out to end of track during the day. Instead, he slipped out of the train long before midnight, bid Kelly's new guards a pleasant good evening, hinted to them that he was headed for a rendezvous with a lady at the Emerald Palace, and then went directly to the livery stable. He saddled the big bay stallion, slipped his rifle into the saddle scabbard, and led the snorting horse out into the street.

"Come on, pal," Shannon said, mounting the horse. "No sleep for us tonight, I'm afraid. I'll make it up to you tomorrow."

He rode slowly and unobtrusively out of town to the east, then circled around the settlement, and once well clear of Railhead City turned west along the railroad. It was easy going on the right of way, and he made good time for the first few miles. Then, as he drew nearer to end of track, he turned the horse up a convenient cleft that cut into the face of the mountain alongside the track and began to climb up toward the top of the ridge, urging the bay stallion through the difficult ascent. At length they reached a narrow plateau halfway up the mountain, and he proceeded along this through the night hours. The moon was setting, but the night was clear and the stars bright. Looking down the mountain slope as he rode, he could see the gleaming ribbon of the railroad tracks far below him, and beyond the tracks, almost lost in the deep, winding canyon, the turbulent white waters of the river rushing past.

Shannon was gambling now, gambling that he had correctly divined the purpose of both the dynamite theft and the firebomb attack on Morgan's dining car. If he was right, someone had used the firebomb to encourage Morgan to take his private train up to end of track, as Morgan had already hinted publicly that he would do. And the only logical purpose of wanting Morgan and his train to move out of Railhead City was to expose it to another attack, this time with the stolen explosives.

The problem, Shannon thought as the horse moved forward over the rocky ground, *is to figure out where the attack will come.* He knew that the explosives could have been set anywhere along the rails above Railhead City, but blowing the track itself would be of little value, since that could be repaired by the track gangs within an hour or two. On the other hand, if the object was the train itself, the best spot for the ambush would be at end of track. There the train would be stopped, and consequently an easy target, because the timing of the fuses would not be so critical. Furthermore, the train would be surrounded by workers then, so that an explosion would involve heavy loss of life. *So I'm betting that will be the place. But if I'm wrong, and they hit somewhere else, a lot of people could die. Please, please let me make the right choice.*

At last, in the hour before dawn, he found himself looking down at end of track. Even in the dim light he could clearly see the log barrier at the end of the rails, the empty roadbed stretching beyond, and the litter strewn along the right-of-way that always seemed to mark the end of the previous day's work. He dismounted and tied the bay securely to a tree, then gave the horse some water and grain that he had brought along for the animal. While the bay munched contentedly, Shannon moved along the ridge, scouting out the ground to find a spot from which he could best observe the activity below.

If they're going to do it here, they'll have to light the fuse from somewhere down there, overlooking the track. I'll have to locate them before they do.

He moved cautiously now, trying not to make any noise or dislodge any rocks that might bounce down the hill. The attackers could already be in place, in which case he must not alarm them.

He took up a position on a rocky outcropping and waited there in the darkness. Just as the first streak of pale gray appeared in the eastern sky, he detected movement below him—scuffling sounds and muted voices. Then he heard what sounded like a shovel digging into loose rock, followed by a low-voiced argument over something, then more scuffling.

They're planting the dynamite right below me. They're not going to blow up the work train, they're going to try to bring half the mountain down on it when it stops. I've got to get to them before the train arrives.

Shannon began to move carefully down the slope, hardly daring to breathe lest the dynamiters should hear him coming. The eastern sky was lighter now, and abruptly the mournful sound of a train whistle echoed through the canyon. Then the huffing of a steam engine laboring up the grade reached his ears, and he heard excited whispers from the enemy below. The unmistakable sound of boots scrambling over stones reached Shannon, and he realized with a start that the men below him were climbing up the hillside, headed directly toward him.

They've finished planting the dynamite, and now they're running the fuse up the hill.

He moved behind some big rocks and waited.

As the first rays of the morning sun reached into the canyon, the work train came wheezing into sight around the last bend. Two of Morgan's three private cars—the dining car and Morgan's office car—were coupled at the tail end of the work train. The locomotive eased to a stop just short of the log barrier, and Shannon saw that Morgan's coaches had been halted directly below him—and directly below the place where the dynamite apparently had been planted.

On the slope below Shannon, two men came into sight, climbing up through the boulders, unreeling rolls of fuse behind them as they came. They stopped on a flat rock overlooking the train, not twenty feet below the spot where Shannon was kneeling.

The sun was well up now, and workmen were pouring off the flatcars of the work train, milling about, sorting out their tools, preparing to begin the day's labors.

"Hurry up, Hank," one of the men on the rock below Shannon said to the other. "Let's fire this off while all those gandy dancers are still milling around the train."

"Just a minute," the second man said. "I got to cut the fuse. Okay, I got it. Let's light it up and get out of here. I want to be in the next county when this one pops."

The first man pulled a match out of his shirt pocket and scratched it across the handle of his revolver. The match flared into life.

Shannon stood up, sliding the Colt revolver out of its holster and stepping into full view of the men on the rock below him.

"Good morning, gentlemen," he said pleasantly. "I'd be obliged if you would raise your hands and step back away from that fuse. Otherwise I'll have to take unpleasant measures that will almost certainly involve the loss of a great deal of your blood."

They gawked at him, open-mouthed. The man with the burning match cursed and dropped it, shaking his scorched fingers vigorously.

"Where the devil did *you* come from?" he squealed.

"Out of your worst nightmare. So back away from that fuse, or die lying next to it. Your choice."

The men backed away.

"Now the gunbelts," Shannon said. "On the ground, slowly, no tricks."

They unbuckled their gunbelts and let them fall.

Keeping the Colt leveled at them, Shannon climbed down to the rock where they were standing. Still keeping them covered, he bent over and tossed the ends of the two unlit fuses over the edge of the cliff so that they slid out of sight below.

"All right, gentlemen," Shannon said, "let's take a walk. There are some people down there on the tracks who are going to be very unhappy over what you were about to do to them."

With the two dynamiters slipping and sliding ahead of him, Shannon made his way down the hill. The railroad crews regarded them curiously as they navigated the last few feet of the incline and started across the roadbed toward the train.

Pat Kelly was the first to reach them.

"What's all this, then, boyo?" he said. "These lads look like they're real tired of holding their hands in the air like that."

"They're a present for Morgan," Shannon said. "They were about to blow him, his train, his track, and all of you to Kingdom Come."

Several of Kelly's train guards came running up, rifles and shotguns at the ready.

"I'd appreciate it if your men would keep an eye on these two for a minute," Shannon said to Kelly. "We have some unfinished business on the mountain. If you can spare a couple of people, I've got a little errand for them to do up there."

"I'll give you all the people you need," Kelly said, glancing suspiciously at the slope. "What's the job?"

"There are two cases of dynamite sitting up there,

right above our heads, ready to drop some very large rocks down on us, and I'd rather the explosives were disarmed by somebody who knows what they're doing. Can you send some of your blasting crew up there to pull the fuses safely and bring the dynamite down here?"

"Pete," Kelly said, turning to a man standing near him, "high-tail it up the track and get the blasting crew back here. Hurry." Pete went sprinting away along the track.

Arthur Holloway came scurrying up, looking even unhappier than usual.

"Mr. Morgan wants to know what's going on," he said.

Shannon looked over at the track, where Morgan's private coach sat just a few yards from him. Morgan was at the window, looking out at them. Shannon waved, and Morgan waved back.

"I'll talk to him myself," Shannon said. He nodded to the guards who were holding their guns on the dyna-miters. "Keep them covered," he said, "but don't hurt them—yet. After I talk with Mr. Morgan, I've got a few questions to ask them."

"We'll hogtie 'em and toss 'em on a flatcar," one of the guards said. "Come on, you maggots. *Move!*"

Two members of the blasting crew came running along the right of way toward them. Kelly explained the situation and sent them scrambling up the hill to retrieve the dynamite.

"One more favor, Pat, if you don't mind," Shannon said to Kelly. "My horse is tied to a tree up there on the first ridge, right above the train. While I'm talking to

Mr. Morgan, could you get someone up there to bring him down? He must be getting a little lonely by now."

"I'll get him," Holloway said.

"Why, thank you," Shannon said, surprised. "That's very decent of you." *Too decent,* he added to himself. *What are you up to, Arthur?*

Holloway had started to move up the track away from the train. Shannon stopped him. "He's right up there," he said, pointing toward the area where he had left the bay. "Directly above us."

"I know," said Holloway over his shoulder. "There's an easier way up just a few yards further along here."

"Gettin' mighty helpful all of a sudden, ain't he?" Kelly observed.

"And very nervous. I wonder why."

"Maybe he's allergic to dynamite," Kelly suggested, grinning.

"Aren't we all?" Shannon said, still watching Holloway's departing figure. "Well, I'd better make my report to Morgan."

In the private car, Shannon explained to Isaac Morgan what he had discovered.

"This is monstrous," Morgan said. "Dozens of people could have been killed."

"Including you," Shannon pointed out. "Your family too."

"Oh, they didn't come with me. My wife insisted on spending the day in town. They're coming up this afternoon—I left the sleeping car to be brought up with a second work train."

"Where's Dalton?" Shannon asked, noting the absence of the railroad's vice-president.

"He's coming up on the second train too. He said he felt he ought to stay with the women to make sure they weren't in any danger."

"Nice of him," Shannon muttered.

Their conversation was interrupted by the sound of gunshots echoing off the canyon walls.

"That came from the hill," Shannon said, heading for the door. He found Kelly and a dozen other men standing by the tracks, craning their necks upward.

"What's going on, Pat?" Shannon asked as he came up.

"Don't know," Kelly said. "Maybe . . ."

Dirt and small rocks suddenly began cascading down the slope, and one of the blasting crew that Kelly had sent up to defuse the dynamite came sliding headfirst down. He collapsed in a heap at their feet, gasping for breath. Shannon saw that he was bleeding from a bullet wound in his side.

"Somebody's up there!" the man panted. "We were just getting ready to pull the fuses on those cases of dynamite when he jumped us. He plugged Mike and then winged me."

"Who was it?" Shannon demanded.

"Don't know. Tall guy, suit. Never saw his face. When he shot me I fell into the rocks below where the explosives are, and all I could see of him was his back as he bent over the boxes. He cut the fuses short with a knife, and then struck a match. Kelly, *he's lighting the fuses on that dynamite!*"

"Saints preserve us!" Kelly cried. "Are you sure?"

"I saw him. He's lit 'em. They're burning right now."

"How short did he cut the fuses?" Shannon said, his

mind racing. The stranger, whoever he was, would have had to cut the fuses long enough to give himself time to get away.

"Real short," the injured blaster wheezed. "About eighteen inches from the blasting caps."

"Quick, Pat," Shannon said. "How long have we got?"

"Burns about a foot a minute," Kelly said. His normally ruddy face was pale.

Shannon felt suddenly pale too. It had taken the wounded blaster at least sixty seconds to get down the hill to warn them.

"Get everybody away from the train!" Shannon shouted. "Drop everything and get as far up the right of way as you can! We're going to have a couple of thousand tons of rocks in our laps in about half a minute! Pat, get that wounded man out of here! Hurry! I'll help Morgan!"

In response to the shouted orders of Kelly and his men, the workers were scattering up and down the track like chickens in a hurricane. Shannon raced back to Morgan's coach and burst in without ceremony.

Morgan's valet, Wimble, was there, looking totally bewildered.

"Help me get Mr. Morgan off the train!" Shannon barked at him. "Come on, Wimble, move! Let's get this wheelchair down the steps!"

They had just started to pick up the wheelchair when suddenly a violent explosion rocked the canyon. The first blast was followed by an earth-shaking rumble that grew rapidly louder as it approached the track.

Shannon cursed.

"Too late! It's an avalanche! Wimble, get Morgan down on the floor and hang on!"

The rumble became a mighty roar as the side of the mountain came hurtling down toward the train. The coach swayed violently on its springs as tons of rocks cascaded across the railroad right of way and began crashing into the coach's sides. The noise was deafening. A window shattered, and dust swirled into the coach, choking them.

And still the horrible roaring continued, as more rocks slid across the tracks and struck the coach. Shannon could hear wood splintering, and he thought for a moment that the car was going to tip over. However, at the last moment the coach righted itself and sat there on the track, vibrating slightly on its trucks like some terrified animal shaking itself.

And then the noise stopped.

Shannon scrambled to his feet.

"Are you all right, Morgan?" he asked, helping the railroad owner back into his wheelchair.

"I'm fine," Morgan said, spitting dust. "Go and see about the others."

The scene outside the coach was surreal. Debris was piled up against the side of the coach, but Shannon saw immediately that the brunt of the avalanche had struck further up the train. A hundred feet of track lay buried under dirt and rock, and one of the workers' flatcars had been flipped over on its back, pulling two other cars off the track with it. At the periphery of the rock slide, men were lying or sitting on the ground, dazed and bloodied, some of them calling for help. Other workers who had been able to get clear in time were running back to the train to assist them.

Shannon walked up the trackside, climbing over the

pile of debris that inundated the track and looked about him at the chaos.

As he did so, emotions flooded through him. First came boiling anger at the destruction. But this was followed quickly by something far worse—a sense of abject failure. All of his plans had gone for nothing. He had done everything right, guessed the point of attack, laid a trap, and sprung it successfully. But someone, some unknown person hiding on the mountain undetected by him, had crept in, set off the dynamite, and changed Shannon's triumph into rancorous, costly disaster. With the taste of gall in his mouth, he began to help the injured and clear away some of the rubble.

Pat Kelly appeared, his face covered with dirt and a cut on his scalp.

"How bad is it, Pat?" Shannon asked. "How many men did we lose?"

"Ah, well, that's the good news, boyo. We've got some cracked heads and an infernal mess on our hands, but it looks like the only men killed in the avalanche were those two you brought down from the mountain. They were tied up on the flatcar that got flipped over."

"Well, I suppose there's some poetic justice in that," Shannon said bitterly. "I just wish that piece of slime up there on the cliff who lit those fuses could have been blown right off the mountain along with those rocks, but I suppose he was well clear before the big bang. What about the other blaster, the first one he shot?"

"He's dead. Bullet through his heart, poor man. His body came down with the slide. We found him just a minute ago."

"Then it's murder after all. There'll be a hanging for this, Pat. I'll find the scum who did this day's work if it takes the rest of my life."

As the workers began to clear away the dirt and rocks from the track, Holloway came hurrying down the right of way leading Shannon's bay horse.

"I was just untying your horse when I heard the explosion," he said breathlessly. "It went off right below me!" He looked around, his expression dazed. "This is terrible. What are we going to do?"

"Never mind that," said Shannon, gazing suspiciously at him. "Did you see anyone moving around up there while you were getting the horse?"

"No, not a soul," Holloway said, fidgeting with the horse's reins. "The first thing I knew about it was when I heard the explosion."

"Considering how many people were on that mountain at the time, it's strange that you didn't see anyone. Maybe you need new glasses, Arthur."

As the workers were clearing away the debris from the side of Morgan's office car, a mournful whistle from down the track signaled the arrival of the second train. It came chugging up the grade from Canyon City and eased to a stop a few yards away from the lower edge of the rockslide. Velda and Amy Morgan disembarked and stood staring, wide-eyed, at the destruction.

"What happened?" Amy said.

"Yes, what's the meaning of all this?" Velda demanded.

Shannon told them.

"Isaac's all right," he added at the end of his narra-
tive. He noted that neither Velda nor Amy had asked
about their husband and father.

Shannon glanced around. Someone was conspicu-
ously missing from the gathering.

"Where's Dalton?" he asked.

"He'll be here later," Amy said.

"Oh?" said Shannon.

"That's correct," Velda Morgan sniffed. "He's coming up on horseback, just as you did last evening."

It was not until much later that it occurred to
Shannon to wonder how Velda knew that he had ridden
a horse up to end of track the previous night.

The work crews spent the day clearing the dirt and
broken rock off the track and levering the derailed cars
back on the rails. They briefly tried to do the same for
the overturned flat car, but it was damaged beyond
repair. Sweating and blaspheming, a hundred workmen
pushed it unceremoniously over the side of the canyon
into the river gorge, where it lay, broken and soon to be
forgotten, on the rocks above the river.

With many hands helping, by mid-afternoon they
had the track clear once again. The bodies of the two
men who had planted the dynamite were laid out on one
of the flatcars. Shannon asked the workers to try to
identify the men, but no one would admit to knowing
them. The body of the blaster who had been shot on the
hillside was wrapped in a blanket and gently laid beside
the other two corpses.

Just as they were finishing the cleanup, Russell
Dalton arrived, riding a tired horse. Shannon noted that

Dalton's clothes were dirty, and his pants leg was torn.

"Good timing," Shannon said to him. "What happened to you?"

"What do you mean? I just rode up from Railhead City."

"I mean your suit. It's a little the worse for wear."

Dalton shrugged. "I fell off my horse," he said, not meeting Shannon's eyes.

"How many times?" Shannon inquired solicitously.

"That's not funny, Shannon. It's none of your concern anyway."

Shannon took Dalton over to the flatcar where the unknown dead men were laid out.

"Do you recognize these people?" Shannon asked, watching Dalton closely.

"No," Dalton said, not looking at the corpses.

"Are you sure? I thought they might be friends of yours."

"Never saw them before in my life," Dalton retorted sulkily. "Now, if you don't mind, I'm going to my compartment to clean up." He gave Shannon a withering glance and went off to the sleeping car, leaving his horse standing untethered on the track.

At the time of the dynamite explosion, the dining car had been coupled behind Morgan's office car, away from the brunt of the rockfall, and as a result had suffered no significant damage. However, dinner was a grim affair, each person lost in his or her own thoughts. Finally, Shannon broke the silence.

"Mr. Morgan," he said, "tomorrow morning I want you to take this train and go back to Railhead City. And this time I want you to stay there. The people who did this thing today were trying to kill you, and they may try again."

Morgan nodded. He lowered his head toward his chest, and when he spoke, his voice was sad, tired, almost defeated.

"Very well, Marshal. Anything you say."

"Why should you do as he says, Isaac?" Holloway blurted. "He didn't do you much good today, did he?"

Morgan raised his head to look at Holloway.

"Arthur," he said, "you're fired."

Holloway gawked at him, speechless.

Velda Morgan leaped up from the table in a frenzy.

"You can't fire him!" she shouted. "You can't fire my brother!"

"Why not?" Morgan asked, his eyes flashing. It was the first time Shannon had seen him angry. "Your dear brother is supposed to be in charge of security, yet from the beginning he and his men have failed to protect this railroad. Failed miserably. His guards let the train be firebombed, they didn't prevent the theft of the dynamite, and while Marshal Shannon has been risking his life repeatedly to help us, all your dear Arthur has done is dither about and whine about how badly he's treated. I've had enough."

"And I've had enough of you," Velda Morgan spat. "You . . . you cripple!"

She ran out of the dining car, sobbing.

"Now, see here, Isaac," Dalton said, his face flushed. "You can't talk to Velda that way. I won't . . ."

"Shut up, Russell," Morgan said. "Before I start asking you where you were today."

Dalton paled. "What do you mean?"

"You know what I mean. Were you up on that hillside this morning, or were you in some dirty hotel in Railhead City with Velda?"

"Wait a minute, Isaac," Dalton sputtered. "You've got me all wrong."

"No, I don't. I know all about you and Velda. When we get back to Railhead City, you can keep going east. With or without my wife."

"Now you just hold it right there!" Dalton shouted. "You can't fire me. I've got a stake in this railroad too. I'm a stockholder. And I'm your vice-president. I'm entitled to—"

"Entitled to what?" Morgan interrupted, his eyes like flint. "To take over as president when I'm through? You can forget that, Russell. That isn't going to happen."

Dalton left the dining car in Velda's wake, cursing vehemently.

"Daddy," Amy said with tears in her eyes, "how could you talk to Mother and Russell that way?" She too jumped up from the table and went running out of the car. Holloway gave Morgan and Shannon a venomous look and followed her.

Shannon had watched all of this with ill-concealed astonishment. He had never expected the calm, cool Morgan to produce such an outburst.

"Well, Mr. Shannon," Morgan said to him when they had all gone, "I apologize to you for the ugly scene you've just witnessed. I'm a bit edgy tonight, and perhaps I shouldn't have spoken so harshly to them. Tomorrow I suppose I'll be sorry that I did, and I'll apologize to them. And then they'll just go on being what they are—worse luck."

Shannon shook his head.

"Family matters are not my affair, Mr. Morgan. But this situation goes far beyond just a family quarrel. I might as well tell you now that there is some evidence that every one of the people who just left this dining car are involved in some way in what's been happening to this railroad lately. I wanted to wait until I had more concrete evidence before distressing you with my suspicions, but after today I think it's time that all the cards were put on the table."

"You think they're *all* involved?" Morgan said slowly. "All of them?"

"Yes. And tomorrow when we get back to Railhead City, I'm telegraphing the territorial capital and getting some deputies up here. This isn't just a railroad matter anymore, Mr. Morgan. Murder has been done, again and again, and it's time a few people started paying for it—whoever they may be."

Morgan's chin sank to his chest again, and he closed his eyes.

"Very well, Marshal. Do what you wish."

He rang for the servant.

"If you'll excuse me, Clay, I'm very tired and I'd like to go to bed. Perhaps we can talk further in the morning."

Shannon went up the track to find Pat Kelly.

"I want double guards on the train tonight, Pat, especially Mr. Morgan's coaches. I know your people are all dead tired, but I've got a bad feeling about this situation and I want to take every possible precaution until we're safely out of here tomorrow. Can you arrange the extra men?"

"I'll take care of it, boyo," Kelly said. "I'll have my crew all around this train, and I'll make sure they stay awake, too, no matter how tired they are."

"Good man, thank you."

Shannon boarded the train again and went into the sleeping car. As he opened the door and entered the car, he discovered Velda Morgan and Russell Dalton standing close together in the corridor, deep in conversation. They looked up as Shannon came down the corridor toward them, and Shannon decided that if looks could kill, he would be a dead man twenty times over.

Shannon nodded to them politely, then entered his compartment and closed the door behind him, glad to be free of their hate-filled glares.

Shortly after two A.M., Shannon came awake, alerted by a faint sound in the corridor. As he watched, the handle of the locked door to his sleeping compartment began to turn, slowly and silently. The handle reached its farthest point of travel, then eased back to its original position. Shannon seized the Colt from the holster hanging beside his berth, unlocked the door, and yanked it open. There was no one there. He checked both ends of the corridor, but it was empty. Descending the steps of the car, he encountered two of Kelly's guards.

"Anyone enter or leave the car?" he asked them.

"Nossir," said the first guard. "Quiet as the grave out here. Anything wrong?"

"I hope not," Shannon said.

He went back to his compartment, relocked the door, and lay down again, still listening. There were no further sounds, but it was a long time before he was able to get back to sleep.

Chapter Twelve
The Horror

"Marshal! Marshal!"

For a moment Shannon thought he was back in the hotel in Railhead City, and that it was the desk clerk, Maxwell, pounding on his door. But as he came awake in the darkened train's sleeping compartment, Shannon realized where he was, and that there was an urgency in the voice outside his door that he had never heard in Maxwell's.

He swung out of the berth and opened the compartment door. Arthur Holloway was standing there, and even in the dim light of the corridor lamp Shannon could see that he was pale as a ghost.

"What is it, Arthur?" Shannon asked wearily.

"It's Mr. M-M-Morgan," Holloway stammered.

"What about Mr. Morgan, Arthur?"

"He's . . . he's dead."

Shannon felt as if someone had just punched him in the stomach.

142

"Dead? Are you sure?"

"Yes. He's *dead*, I tell you."

Shannon saw Holloway was literally quaking with fear.

"Calm down, Arthur, where is he?"

"In his sleeping compartment. Please come at once."

Shannon hastily pulled on his clothes, glancing at his watch as he did so. It was a little past five o'clock. Dawn in less than an hour.

"Hurry!" Holloway said.

"Why?" Shannon shot back angrily, buckling his gunbelt. "If he's dead, there isn't any hurry, is there?"

A crowd had gathered around the door of Morgan's sleeping compartment. Shannon pushed through without ceremony. One of the compartment lamps was lit, and by its dim light Shannon saw Isaac Morgan lying in his berth, his body unnaturally still, his eyes wide open as they gazed unblinkingly at a ceiling that he could not see.

Shannon bent over the body to check for a pulse, but even as he touched Morgan's throat he felt the stiffness of the muscles and he knew immediately that there would be no pulse to check.

His shoulders sagged. The final defeat, the ultimate and irretrievable failure, was upon him. Cold fury filled his heart as he turned toward the figures crowded together in the doorway.

"Who found him?"

"I did, sir," said the manservant, Wimble. "I came in and he was like that, just as you see him."

"What were you doing in his compartment at five o'clock in the morning?"

"He told me last night to wake him at five, sir. He

almost always gets up at that hour, and he said that he particularly wanted to be up by that time this morning."

Shannon looked searchingly at the faces in the corridor. Wimble, dazed and shaking. Holloway, his cheeks drained of color. Amy Morgan, looking defiantly back at him, her eyes dry and hard. At the rear, Russell Dalton, staring past Shannon at the corpse with a complete lack of expression. And at the front, Velda Morgan, calm, haughty, and with a triumphant smile on her lips.

I'm sorry, Morgan, Shannon thought. *You were a good man, but you lived in a nest of vipers, and you died in it—unloved and alone. How sad. How very, very sad.* And then it occurred to him that he too was now alone in the same vipers' nest.

"Holloway, go get Pat Kelly," he said.

"I don't want a common Irish laborer in this coach," Velda Morgan huffed.

"Get him, Arthur," Shannon said. Holloway hesitated, looking at Velda.

"Go get him, Arthur!" Shannon barked. *"Now!"*

Holloway hurried away toward the end of the car.

Kelly arrived, his face set and hard as he looked down at his late employer. Shannon was lighting the other lamps in the compartment.

"Close the door behind you, will you, Pat?" Shannon said.

Reluctantly, the others allowed themselves to be shut out of the compartment.

When he and Kelly were alone, Shannon sat down on the edge of the bunk to examine the body.

"Sorry to have to bring you in on this, Pat," he said, "but I want a witness here that I can trust."

"How did he die?" Kelly said, still staring at the corpse.

"I don't know. That's what we're going to try to find out."

Carefully, Shannon pulled back the covers and began to inspect the corpse. There were no wounds, no blood on the sheets or pillow, no signs of violence at all. Shannon sniffed at the dead man's lips, but there was no froth or odor of poison. There was a very small cut on Morgan's lower lip, but it was obviously superficial, and there was no visible bleeding, bruising, or swelling.

"He's been dead for several hours," Shannon said. "Rigor mortis has already set in." He turned the body halfway over in the berth and pulled back the edge of Morgan's silk nightshirt. "Lividity," Shannon said, pointing to the dark patches on the skin.

"What's that?" Kelly asked, blinking.

"After a person is dead, gravity causes blood to settle to the parts of the body that are lowest. That takes time, like rigor mortis. He's been dead for at least four or five hours, and from what I can tell, he died right here—there's no indication that the body's been moved."

He opened the buttons at the neck of Morgan's nightshirt and inspected the dead man's throat.

"No signs of strangulation, and certainly no indication from the features that he was suffocated. Did he have any illnesses that you know of, Pat? Aside from the paralysis of his legs, I mean."

"Not as I know of. The family would know, I suppose."

"They'd know, but at this point I wouldn't believe anything they told me."

Kelly eyes were wide.

"You think one of *them* killed him?"

"If they did, they did it in some way that I can't discover," Shannon said. "At least I can't discover it in this compartment in a narrow berth in the middle of the night by the light of a couple of smoking oil lamps."

He reached over and gently closed Morgan's eyelids. Then he pulled the sheet up over the dead man's face.

"Pat, get the train crew to couple Morgan's private coach and the dining car onto this train, so that all three private coaches are together again. Then tell the engineer to get up steam and start back to Railhead City immediately. Tell him that I want this train moving at full throttle in fifteen minutes. And tell him that if it isn't, I'll throw him off the footplate and drive the engine back to town myself."

As Kelly departed to find the train crew, Shannon stepped back into the corridor and closed the door. The vipers were still there, waiting.

"What did you find out, Marshal?" Holloway asked anxiously. "What killed him?"

"Don't be an ass, Arthur," Velda Morgan said. "Obviously it was a heart attack."

"Perhaps," Shannon said, "we'll see."

Kelly was back within a few minutes. Outside, the voices of the train crew, the clash of metal on metal, and the sudden jerking of the sleeping car told Shannon that the preparations were underway for the return journey.

"What's going on out there?" Velda demanded, staring hostilely at Shannon.

"We're going back to Railhead City," Shannon said.

The car lurched again, and then began to move.

"But what about Isaac?" Holloway asked.

"I thought we'd take him with us, if that's all right with you," Shannon replied caustically.

"Of course, but I mean, what do we do now?"

"First of all, as soon as we get to Railhead City, I'm going to send for Dr. Lin and have him examine Mr. Morgan's body."

"Absolutely not!" Velda snorted. "I won't have any filthy foreigner touching my husband, doctor or not."

"Spare me your stupid prejudices, Mrs. Morgan. I don't have time for them right now."

"Now just a minute, Shannon," Russell Dalton began. "I'm the vice-president of this railroad, and . . ."

"Be quiet, Russell," Velda said. "I'll do the talking here."

She stepped forward and pointed an angry finger at Shannon.

"Mr. Shannon," she hissed, "I don't like your attitude. I agree that we should go back to Railhead City, but you just remember this—with my husband gone, I own the majority interest in this railroad. I'm in charge here now, and when we reach town I'll say what will be done and won't be done."

"You're wrong, Mrs. Morgan," Shannon said, folding his arms and leaning against the closed door of the dead man's compartment. "You're not in charge here. I am. Until I know whether your husband's death was natural or not, this entire train will be treated as a crime scene, and I'll do as I think fit with it."

He turned to the others.

"Go back to your compartments and stay there until we reach Railhead City. When we get there, you are to remain on the train until I say otherwise. Is that clear?"

There was a rumble of dissension in the group, but no one challenged him again. With surly glances back at Shannon, and still grumbling to themselves and each other, they shuffled away toward their own compartments.

At Shannon's request, Pat Kelly had reboarded the train and was waiting at the end of the corridor.

"I put all the men who were guarding the train last night into the dining car," Kelly said.

"Good. Let's go talk to them."

But none of Kelly's men had seen or heard anything. As far as they knew, no one had boarded or gotten off the train during the night.

"No help there," Kelly grumbled. "What now?"

"I don't know, Pat," Shannon said. "Something killed Morgan, and to find out what it was I'm going to need some medical assistance."

"You mean Doctor Lin? If you let Lin anywhere near Morgan's body, old Velda's gonna have apoplexy."

"What a shame," Shannon said.

"Another half-hour," Kelly said, checking his watch.

He and Shannon were sitting in Shannon's compartment on the sleeping car. Shannon had sent the others to the office car to get them out of the way, but he wanted to remain where he could keep an eye on Morgan's corpse.

The gorge was widening out as they approached the small valley that had become Railhead City, and trees now lined the track instead of sheer rock walls.

Shannon glanced out the window just in time to see five riders burst out of the woods, firing their rifles at the train. Shannon heard the sound of breaking glass and the thud of bullets burying themselves in wood.

"Come on," he said, drawing his revolver. "They're firing at Morgan's private car."

They ran into the office car to find all of its occupants cowering on the floor beneath the windows. Amy Morgan was sobbing in terror, and Holloway looked as if he was about to faint. Dalton and Velda Morgan were pale, but their expressions as they looked up at Shannon from the floor were almost blank.

Several more rifle bullets struck the outside of the coach, and one whirred through the broken window to lodge itself in the mahogany paneling over Morgan's desk.

Shannon crouched beside the window and looked out. The five horsemen were galloping beside the train, shooting into the coach. Shannon took careful aim with his .45 and fired, knocking one of the riflemen out of the saddle. At the same time, Kelly's guards opened fire from the windows of the dining car, hitting two more of the attackers. The remaining two riders pulled their horses to a rapid halt, took one quick look back at their fallen comrades, and then put their mounts into a dead run toward the tree line.

"Looks like somebody's still trying to kill Morgan," Kelly said. "Guess whoever they were, they don't know yet that Morgan's dead."

"Either that, or they weren't trying for Morgan," Shannon said. "It might have been just more harassment of the railroad."

He holstered the Colt.

"You can get up now, friends," he said. "The big bad men have gone."

"No need for sarcasm, Shannon," Dalton said, standing up and brushing bits of shattered glass off his trousers. "We could have been killed. Velda and Amy were very frightened."

"Ladies," Shannon said, bowing elaborately to the two women on the floor, "you have my *deepest* sympathy."

They pulled into the railroad yard at Railhead City a few minutes later. Scotty, the engineer who had been driving the locomotive, came hurrying back to the coach.

"I'm sorry, Mr. Dalton," he cried, "but when those men started shooting at the train, I figured the best thing to do was to keep going and try to outrun them."

"You did fine, Scotty," Shannon said. "You can go now."

"Blast it, Shannon," Dalton said, "you can't keep giving my employees orders. I'm the vice-president, remember."

"Well, Mr. Vice-President," Shannon said, "you can take it as an order or not, as you please, but I want you and the rest of your little group to stay here in the coach for a while. I need to discuss a few things with you."

"You have no right to hold us here," Velda Morgan said. "My husband died of a heart attack, and that's that. So I'm taking my things and getting off this train right now, and you can't stop me."

As frustrating as it was, Shannon knew that Velda was right. He had not one shred of evidence to show that Isaac Morgan had died of anything but natural causes, and in any event it was obvious that none of these people were going to tell him anything of value, no matter how long he questioned them.

"Very well, Mrs. Morgan," Shannon said, temporarily defeated. "But none of you are to leave Canyon City until I say so. Now, where can I find you if I have further need for you?"

"I don't know about anyone else," Velda said haughtily, "but I'm going to that nasty wooden hotel in the center of town. At least they have a bathtub there."

When the others had left the train, Holloway lingered behind.

"I didn't kill him, you know," he said to Shannon in a small voice. "It wasn't me."

"What makes you think he was killed? I thought he was supposed to have died of a heart attack."

"There wasn't anything wrong with his heart," Holloway said, staring fixedly at the carpet.

"Come on, Arthur. If you know something, let's have it."

Holloway shook his head violently and fled from the coach.

Dr. Lin boarded the sleeping car with his aged servant trailing at a respectful distance.

"Thank you for coming," Shannon said, escorting Lin to Morgan's sleeping compartment. "I know it's a great imposition, but I need your help badly. I'm not a doctor, and I need a medical opinion on this matter."

"I am glad to be of assistance," Lin said, folding his hands into his wide sleeves. "How can I help you?"

Shannon told him the story. Aided by the bright sunlight streaming through the window of Morgan's compartment, Dr. Lin conducted a minute examination of the body.

"Mr. Morgan's family were right," he said at length, turning to Shannon with a quizzical smile.

"You mean he died of a heart attack?" Shannon said, dumbfounded. He could not believe that all of his instincts had been so wrong.

"Yes. But the heart attack was not a natural occurrence. Please to look here."

He touched Morgan's chest with the tip of one of his long fingernails. Shannon drew a sharp breath. In the center of Morgan's chest, so tiny as to be almost invisible, was a minute mark on the skin. It was so small that Shannon had not even seen it in the dim light of the compartment the previous night. Gingerly, he touched the mark and then held his finger up to the window. Adhering to his fingertip were a few tiny crystals of a dark brown substance that Shannon knew could be only dried blood. He looked at Lin questioningly.

"Yes," Dr. Lin said. "Someone has driven a very small, very sharp object into Mr. Morgan's heart."

"Too small to be a knife," Shannon said. "A needle of some kind, perhaps?"

"Certainly nothing larger than that. But your suspicions were correct, Mr. Shannon. Your friend was murdered, and in a very cold-blooded way."

"He must have been asleep at the time. Someone entered the compartment and drove the needle, or whatever it was, into his heart, killing him."

"So it would seem," Dr. Lin said.

Shannon scowled.

"But with such a small weapon," he said, "surely death wouldn't have been instantaneous. Even assuming that he was asleep when the killer entered the compartment, wouldn't Morgan have had time to cry out as the needle penetrated his chest?"

"Not necessarily," Dr. Lin replied. "By skill or by luck the murder weapon appears to have penetrated at a point that would stop the heart immediately. This might very well have caused Mr. Morgan to lose consciousness without having an opportunity to call out."

"But what if he had? I'd surely have heard him and come to investigate. The killers took a big chance."

"They took no chances at all, Mr. Shannon. Look here."

Lin indicated the small cut on the inside of Morgan's lower lip.

"I noticed it last night," Shannon said, "but it may have been caused by a stone striking Mr. Morgan yesterday morning when the rockslide was hitting the coach. One of the windows broke, and a lot of debris was coming in. Do you think it has something to do with his murder?"

"I think it may be very enlightening," Dr. Lin said.

"But whenever it occurred, surely that little nick isn't enough to have caused Morgan any harm."

"No," Dr. Lin agreed, "the cut itself is minor. But it suggests that someone held a hand tightly over Mr. Morgan's mouth while the weapon was being driven into his heart, thus preventing him from crying out. The pressure of the murderer's hand forcing Mr. Morgan's lips against his teeth was enough to cause the small split in the skin."

Shannon nodded in sudden understanding.

"Of course," he said, mentally chiding himself for not having guessed at it sooner. "There was no bruising or swelling of the lips, because Morgan died immediately, so those things didn't develop."

"Precisely," Dr. Lin said, returning his hands to his sleeves. "Bruising and swelling are caused by bleeding under the skin, and only the living bleed. Mr. Morgan was dead before it could occur."

Shannon fought back a wave of revulsion, picturing the semi-paralyzed Morgan, helpless in his bed, awakening in terror to feel the murderer's hand upon his mouth and the instrument of death already piercing his heart. It was an ugly, painful image, and Shannon strove to erase it from his mind.

"I have to find the weapon," he said. "Without it, I'll never prove which one of them did it. Of course, they may have thrown it away—tossed it out of the window of the train for example—in which case I'll never find it. But I have to try. I just wish I knew exactly what I'm looking for."

"Keep an open mind as you search," Dr. Lin said gravely. "Do not think only of needles. Remember, in the wrong hands, even an ornament can be an instrument of death."

"Any other advice?" Shannon asked hopefully.

"I'm afraid that I can tell you nothing more. And now I must go. I hope that I have been helpful."

When Dr. Lin had left the train, Shannon covered the body with the sheet again and stood up, holding the lamp and looking down at the mortal remains of Isaac Morgan.

Don't worry, Mr. Morgan, they almost got away with it, but not quite. There's a gallows waiting out there for someone now. All I have to do is find out which neck fits the noose.

Chapter Thirteen
The Weakest Link

Sharpened by his anger, Shannon's hunting instincts were now in full cry. For more than an hour he searched through the train, going through the sleeping car, then the diner, and finally Morgan's office coach.

If only I'd known about the needle mark before those people took their things off the train. But that's spilled milk. Let's see what's left.

No evidence of murder came to light, but he did find one curious thing in the drawer of Morgan's desk. It was Morgan's will. The document was dated only a few weeks previously, and it left everything to Morgan's daughter, Amy.

Cut old Velda off without a cent. And hardly a month ago. Well, it's not too surprising—Morgan said last night that he knew his wife was being unfaithful. Too bad, Velda. It looks like you're not going to be in charge after all.

He left the train and hurried through town to the

hotel where he had been staying and to which Velda Morgan had announced that she was going. He found Maxwell, the desk clerk, sleeping on a cot in the office behind the desk.

"Wake up, Maxwell," Shannon said, shaking him. "Did Velda Morgan and the others from the train check in here this morning?"

"Uh, yeah, they did," Maxwell said, yawning.

"Are they in their rooms now?"

"Don't think so. The ladies and Mr. Dalton left to get something to eat. Mr. Holloway went out a while ago, but I don't know where."

"Give me your passkey," Shannon said.

Working rapidly, he searched each of the rooms that had been rented by the passengers from the train, but there was nothing in any of their belongings that would link them in any way to the attacks on the railroad or Morgan's death.

No needles, no knives, no nothing. These people are either innocent or very careful. And I don't think they're innocent. Not one of them.

He went out of the hotel and began walking through the town, hoping that the crisp morning air would help him to organize his thoughts.

It's obviously a conspiracy, and the best way to break any conspiracy is to attack the weakest link. And my guess is that in this case by far the weakest link is Arthur Holloway. Now where is he?

"Good heavens, Clay," Tank Drummond said, wrapping his robe around him as he came out of his sleeping tent. "It's not even noon. Saloon owners have to sleep sometime."

"I'm sorry, Tank," Shannon said, "but you're paying the penalty for knowing everybody in town. Where might I find Arthur Holloway at this hour? Saloon? Girlfriend's place? Gambling hall?"

Drummond looked thoughtful.

"Bit early for it," he said, "but if it were a little later in the day I know where he might be."

The tent was a small one, located deep in the Chinese sector. As Shannon approached, a large man with an axe tucked in his belt stepped out of the tent flap and barred Shannon's way.

"I'm looking for someone," Shannon said. "May I go in?"

"You are the policeman who helped my friend Wei Lee," the man said. "Doctor Lin has told us to help you if we can. You may go in."

The tent was dark, but Shannon could see that there were a number of cots placed around the tent. The men sprawled on them were either asleep or holding pipes in their hands, and the air was thick with the fumes of the opium they were smoking.

Arthur Holloway was on one of the cots near the side of the tent. Shannon knocked the pipe out of his hand, lifted him from the cot, and pushed him unceremoniously out of the tent.

Holloway blinked stupidly in the sunshine, looking about him as if he had suddenly found himself on another planet.

"Come on, Arthur," Shannon said, grabbing him by the belt. "It's time to sober up. After that, it'll be time to sing."

Shannon propelled Holloway down the street to the

Emerald Palace. Tank Drummond volunteered his
sleeping tent and sent over a pot of coffee. There was a
table in the sleeping tent, and Shannon sat Holloway
down in front of it and poured the coffee. Holloway
downed the first cup, then looked up at Shannon, his
bloodshot eyes filled with misery.

"You know, don't you?" he said in a trembling voice.

"Some of it. Now you're going to tell me the rest."

Hesitantly at first, then faster and more eagerly, the
wretched Holloway began to bare his soul.

"There was a plot, all right, but its main goal wasn't
to ruin the railroad. It was to kill Isaac Morgan. They
were all in on it, just as you suspected. Dalton wanted
control of the railroad, but he was just a minority
shareholder. Morgan owned the majority of the stock,
so Dalton had to find a way to get hold of Morgan's
shares. His problem was that if Morgan died, Velda
would inherit Morgan's stock, so Dalton started
romancing Velda. It was easy for him too. You know
what my sister's like, Marshal—vain, self-centered,
enjoys flirting with men. She became infatuated with
Dalton, began having an affair with him. When he had
her thoroughly hooked, he told her about his plan to
get rid of Morgan and take over the railroad. Velda
was greedy for money and power, and she had no further use for Morgan, so she agreed to help Dalton kill
him."

"What exactly was the plan?"

"Dalton's deal with Velda was that when Morgan
was dead, Dalton would marry her. Then they would
have the stock and therefore own the railroad. If they
could finish what Morgan started, driving through the

mountains to the west, they'd have land, money, everything they'd both ever wanted."

"What went wrong?"

"Morgan found out about Dalton and Velda, and
changed his will, leaving everything, including all his
railroad stock, to Amy. Velda didn't know about the
change, but Dalton found out about it. Maybe Morgan
told him, or maybe Dalton just came across the new
will in Morgan's desk. Anyway, after that Dalton had to
rethink his scheme. He kept on with his little charade
with Velda, but he also went after Amy. Being the silly
little fool that she is, she fell head over heels in love
with him. Amy is just as greedy as Velda, and she
despised her father, so when Dalton was sure of her and
disclosed his scheme to her, Amy agreed to help with
the plot. She didn't care about the railroad itself, but
she wanted Dalton and he promised her a life of luxury once Amy had inherited the stock and they had control of the company."

Shannon was becoming slightly dizzy trying to follow all of this.

"So Dalton was having an affair with both Amy and
her mother at the same time," he mused. "That must
have been a little complicated for him. No wonder I
never saw him around the train much. What were they
going to do about Velda when she found out Dalton was
two-timing her?"

"They figured once Morgan was dead, Dalton would
dump Velda or else they'd kill her, just to shut her up.
Then Dalton would marry Amy."

"Didn't it bother Amy at all that after helping to kill

her father, she was going to be a party to the killing of her mother too?"

"Not a bit," Holloway said with evident distaste. "Amy puts on a great act, all childlike and sugary-sweet. But underneath she's as hard as nails, and completely without compassion or principle."

Shannon shuddered, remembering how young and innocent Amy had seemed when he first met her. "So," he said, "since Velda Morgan didn't know about the new will, and didn't know about Dalton's affair with Amy, or their plans to kill her too, Velda continued to help with the plot against Morgan."

"That's it," Holloway said. "Pretty grim, isn't it?"

"It's sickening," Shannon said. "So much malice directed against one decent, unsuspecting man. But what's all this got to do with the attacks on the railroad?"

"That was the flaw in the plan. They realized that if Morgan was murdered, they'd all immediately be suspects. Motive alone would point right to them unless they could find a way to deflect suspicion or, better yet, get someone else to kill Morgan for them. They decided to stage a series of attacks on the railroad, making it look like someone outside Morgan's inner circle was trying to ruin him. Then, using the attacks as cover, they'd have Morgan killed in a way that wouldn't incriminate them. No motive, no suspicion, and they'd be in the clear."

"So how did Kenny Allen get mixed up with Amy? I thought you said she was in love with Dalton."

"She was. Still is, I guess. But they needed outside help. They needed to find someone to carry out the attacks on the railroad for them. What better ally than the rival railroad? The Allen family certainly had a motive to see the Denver & Northern Sierra fail, but Dalton and the others knew that Allen Senior was honest, a man with too much integrity to play foul."

"I see. So they decided to recruit young Kenny."

"Exactly. They knew him for what he is—a gun-happy punk, ambitious, immature, impetuous, cruel—just what they needed."

"So," Shannon said, "with her own mother's blessing as well as her lover's, dear little Amy started romancing Junior, got him smitten with her, and then talked him into helping to sabotage the railroad."

"Yes. Amy didn't tell him of the plan to kill Morgan, of course. She made him believe that the railroad was the only target. I heard them talking one night outside our train. She convinced him that if he could delay the Denver & Northern Sierra enough, his father's railroad would be first through the mountains. Then his father would be rich, and she'd marry Kenny."

"I can see how that would appeal to Junior. He'd get the delectable Amy, and with his father dying of consumption, very soon Kenny would take over the St. Louis, Salt Lake, & Western. They'd have not only that railroad, but since he would be married to Amy, who would inherit the Denver & Northern Sierra, they'd wind up with both railroads, combine them, and live like royalty for the rest of their lives."

"Yeah. And the little puke fell for it, all the way. He hired men to do the dirty work, thinking he was helping his father's railroad and, more importantly, himself. Some of those he hired were ex-railroad men, people who knew something about trains and railroading and could find ways to do the most damage."

"Not all of it was hired out," Shannon said. "Kenny did some of the killing in person, like those laborers that were shot while they were working. And he tried to kill me, first at end of track and then in the woods when I interrupted one of his little trysts with Amy."

"Yeah, your appearance upset their plans considerably. You had them worried right from the moment you got involved. They even had that Indian kid hiding under Morgan's private car the day you arrived, trying to hear what he was telling you. Then, after you cold-shouldered Amy and rejected Dalton's bribe attempt, they hired somebody to try to shoot you in your hotel room that very night."

"I remember," Shannon said dryly. "The price for my life was fifty dollars, as I recall."

"Originally, Dalton and Velda and Amy had figured that they could wait until everyone around them was completely convinced that somebody else was plotting against the railroad, and then they could safely go ahead and kill Morgan. But when you showed up and they couldn't seduce you or bribe you or kill you, they knew they had to move more quickly than they had intended. That's when they got young Allen to set up the dynamite ambush. They thought they'd blow Morgan's car off the track and into the river with him inside, and maybe you too. That's why none of them were at end of track that day—they didn't want to be on the train when the mountain came down on it."

"And that's why you volunteered to go get my

horse—to get yourself out of danger too. Who lit the fuses, you or Dalton?"

"It was Dalton. He'd been trailing the men he'd sent to do the blasting, keeping tabs on them just in case something went wrong. When you stopped them from setting off the explosion, he decided to light the fuses himself. He came running past me as I was on the way up the hill for your horse. I wanted to interfere, but by then it was too late. Besides, he'd have killed me if I'd tried."

"I suppose he would have," Shannon said grudgingly. "He was sure that the dynamite would get both Morgan and me at the same time, and that would have solved all of their problems."

"Yes. But the explosion didn't get you or Morgan, and they realized from what you'd said and done that you now suspected that Dalton and the family were involved, and they guessed that you were getting close to unraveling the whole thing. They panicked, and Velda convinced Dalton they had to go ahead and kill Morgan themselves."

He lowered his face into his hands, and his voice became a whisper.

"I could have stopped it," he went on. "I heard them in the sleeping car corridor last night, talking about it."

Shannon's eyes narrowed, as he recalled interrupting Velda and Dalton in the corridor, and the vitriolic looks they gave him.

"I tried to tell you about it last night," Holloway went on. "I came to your compartment later to talk to you. I couldn't knock for fear they'd hear me, so I just tried the door handle. I was going to come in and tell you everything, but when I couldn't open the door I lost my nerve. I'd gotten so embroiled in their scheme, you see."

"Just how embroiled?" Shannon said.

"Right at the beginning, Velda talked me into helping with their plan, and I agreed to go along because she's my sister, and I was angry at Isaac. I resented the way he treated me, resented just being the brother-in-law that nobody respected. Then you came, and I saw right away that you were smart enough to expose the plot. I wanted out right then, but I was in too deep. I'd helped by weakening security, looking the other way when workers were shot, and so on."

"And you had no qualms about killing Morgan? Seems like your whole family is a little short on conscience."

Tears welled up in Holloway's eyes.

"At the beginning it didn't seem so bad," he sniffled, "some other railroad killing Isaac. But when Dalton and Velda started talking last night about doing it themselves, it made me sick. So I wanted to tell you, but I was afraid you'd arrest me too. I didn't want to go to jail, or hang for what they did. And then there was Velda. If I talked, she'd go to jail or hang too. My sister is an evil woman, Marshal—I see that now. But with all that bearing down on me, I didn't have the courage to tell you. If I had, Isaac Morgan would be alive today."

"So which of them actually killed Morgan?"

"I don't know," Holloway replied, wiping his eyes with his handkerchief. "All I heard was that bit of talk in the corridor. It could have been Dalton, or Velda, or even Amy. Yes, it could have been Amy too. They were all capable of it."

Shannon sat for a time, his chin in his hand, trying to absorb all of this.

"What are you going to do with me?" Holloway asked tearfully.

"I don't know. Right now, I want you to go back to the hotel and wait there until I come to get you. Stay away from the others. If you run into them, don't tell them you've seen me, and whatever you do, don't let them know you've told me all of this."

"Whatever you say, Marshal. I don't really care what happens to me now."

Shannon shadowed Arthur Holloway through the town until he was sure that Holloway was returning to his hotel. Then he began to walk back to the railroad yard.

I must find the murder weapon. Without that, I have no way of proving who actually killed Morgan. But I've been through all of their belongings, and there was nothing that would make that kind of wound.

He stopped suddenly. *What was it that Dr. Lin had said on the train? "Even an ornament may be an instrument of death."*

He turned and raced back to the hotel.

"They come back yet?" he called to Maxwell as he hurried through the lobby.

"Just Mr. Holloway," Maxwell said. "Haven't seen the others."

"If they come in, stall them. Keep them here in the lobby until I'm through in their rooms. You understand?"

"Not exactly," Maxwell said with a puzzled look, "but I'll do my best."

Ten minutes later he found it. On the top shelf of the crude wardrobe closet in Velda Morgan's room was a flowery lady's hat. Protruding from the crown was a four-inch-long hatpin. Shannon withdrew the hatpin from the hat and examined it closely. There were brown stains on the pin. He had found the murder weapon.

Strange, how such a common, ordinary, everyday thing could so savagely end a man's life.

But even as he looked at it, he realized that there was still one problem. He was a careful and observant man, and he knew beyond any doubt that the hatpin had not been in the hat when he had searched the room an hour before.

Anyone with any sense would have thrown this away long ago. But someone not only kept it, they also took the trouble and risk of putting it back into Velda's room. Whoever did it is either being overcautious or trying to deliberately incriminate Velda.

Maxwell was behind the desk when he went back to the lobby.

"Any luck, Marshal?"

"Maxwell, I want you to think very carefully about this. Do you know if anyone has been in Mrs. Morgan's room since the last time I was here?"

"Why, yes. I was helping bring in a couple of new guests' bags about thirty minutes ago and I saw someone coming out of Mrs. Morgan's room."

"Who was it?" Shannon said, hardly daring to breathe.

"Well, I don't like to talk about the guests' business. Besides, I've seen him going in and out of Mrs. Morgan's room before when she stayed here."

"Never mind the desk clerk union's oath of silence, Maxwell. Just tell me who it was, please."

"It was Mr. Dalton."

Shannon felt as if a great weight had been lifted from his shoulders.

I've got my case, now. With Holloway's testimony, I can put a noose around several necks, including Dalton's.

Borrowing a piece of paper, he wrote out a message and handed it to Maxwell.

"Have you got somebody here who could take this down to the telegraph office?"

"Sure," said Maxwell. "I'll take it myself. Gosh, this is to the territorial governor."

"Yes. Make sure it gets sent immediately, will you? Here's the money. And while you're there, find out if there's a telegram for me from my wife—I still haven't heard from her, and I'm worried. Now, I know that Arthur Holloway came in a while ago. Is he still in his room?"

"I guess so. Haven't seen him leave. He was really upset when he came in."

"I'll bet he was," Shannon said unsympathetically.

"He was crying, Marshal, crying like a baby. I've never seen a man in such a terrible state."

A sudden dark foreboding swept over Shannon.

"Let me have your passkey again." Snatching it from the desk clerk's hand, he ran down the corridor to Holloway's room.

"Holloway?" he said, pounding on the door. "You in there?"

There was no answer. Shannon tried the door and

found it locked. He twisted the passkey in the lock and pushed open the door.

Holloway was hanging from the lamp hook on the ceiling, a string tie wound tightly around his neck. He had stood on the chair, knotted the tie around the hook, and then stepped off the chair, strangling himself. Shannon stood there, gazing up at his dead witness, nauseated by the sight.

Lousy way to die, Arthur. You should have waited for the hangman—he'd have done a better job.

There was a scrawled note on the night stand, and Shannon picked it up.

All it said was: *I'm sorry.*

"I'm sorry too, Arthur," Shannon said to the dangling corpse. "I'm sorry for you, and I'm sorry because my case against your murderous friends just died with you."

Chapter Fourteen
Junior

With Holloway's testimony lost, Shannon knew
that he would have to find yet another weak link in
the conspiracy. Who would it be? Not Dalton, not
Velda. Amy? Unlikely. That left only one—Kenny
Allen. But was he in Railhead City? If he had been
involved in the rifle attack on the train that morning,
he might well still be in town, and if he was, odds
were that he was in some saloon gloating over his latest exploit. Consequently, while waiting for Railhead
City's barber to arrive once more to fulfill his role as
undertaker, Shannon again sent Maxwell scurrying
off with a note for the owner of the Emerald Palace
saloon.

As the harried desk clerk left the hotel, Dalton, Velda
Morgan, and Amy Morgan came walking in. Shannon
could hear them laughing as they passed through the
lobby. They stopped short when they saw Shannon
standing in the hallway outside Holloway's room.

"Step right up, folks," Shannon said, beckoning them to the open door. "Take a good look. It'll make you very proud of yourselves."

They peered through the doorway at Holloway's body swinging gently from the lamp hook.

Velda gasped, Amy said "Oh!" and Dalton said nothing at all.

"Is he dead?" Amy asked.

"No," said Shannon sarcastically, "he's just taking a nap in a very strange position."

"Why did the stupid fool do it?" Velda muttered.

"You can ask him next time you see him," Shannon suggested.

Maxwell running up, puffing from his exertions, and handed Shannon a message.

You're in luck. Your pigeon is roosting at my bar.
Drummond

Shannon crumpled up the note and stuck it in his pocket.

"I have to go out now," he said. "I want you three to stay here until I return. Don't try to run for it in the meantime—if you do, I'll find you and drag you back anyway."

"Now see here," Dalton began, "you can't make us stay here if we don't want to."

"Shut up, Dalton," Shannon grated. "I'm not in a good mood right now, so don't push me. Just do what I tell you and I may let you keep your teeth a while longer."

The Emerald Palace was emitting its usual blend of piano music and drunken voices. As Shannon approached the entrance, he noted Kenny Allen's paint horse was tied to the hitch rail once more. There were fresh rowel marks on its sides.

Allen was standing at the bar, downing the contents of a shot glass. A nearly empty bottle of whiskey stood on the bar in front of him. As he raised the shot glass, he looked at the mirror and caught sight of Shannon coming up behind him. He slapped the shot glass on the bar and whirled around, both hands dropping to the handles of his twin six-guns.

Shannon drove his left fist straight into Allen's face, sending him back hard against the edge of the bar. Recovering his balance, Allen made another try for his guns. Shannon drew his Colt and whipped the barrel against Allen's temple, knocking him to the floor. As Allen began trying groggily to regain his feet, Shannon leaned over and dragged first one revolver, then the other from the stunned man's holsters, tossing the weapons over the bar out of Allen's reach. Then he grabbed Allen by the shirt, swung him around, and shoved him hard onto his back on the nearest roulette table. Allen's legs were hanging over the edge of the table, and holding Allen down on the table with one arm, Shannon yanked on the strap of one of Allen's spurs, unbuckling it from his boot. Allen was struggling to break free of Shannon's grasp, squirming and screaming curses, but Shannon now had his elbow on Allen's chest, bearing down with his full weight. Holding the spur firmly in his hand, Shannon leaned over Allen and forced the rowel of the spur between Allen's teeth. He held it there, three inches into Allen's open mouth, and waited. Allen's struggles ceased abruptly, and his eyes grew wide with fear as he felt the sharp points of the spur rowel pressing against his tongue.

"Wade a mint," he mumbled, not daring to move his mouth very far. "Wha ya doon?"

"Just what I said I'd do if I saw blood on that paint horse's side again," Shannon said. "I'm going to shove this spur down your throat. Then I'm going to do the same with the other one. Let me know if it hurts going down, will you?"

"Don' doot! Pliz!"

Tank Drummond was leaning against the bar, watching all of this with interest. Shannon caught his eye and gave him a meaningful nod. Drummond realized immediately what Shannon wanted him to do.

"Now wait, Clay," Drummond said, winking at Shannon. "Be reasonable. The kid wants to cooperate, don't you Kenny?"

"Yah, cupperate," Allen mumbled, still trying not to move his jaw. "Ow, tha hurz ma tung!"

"I don't know, Tank," Shannon growled fiercely. "I sure would enjoy ramming these spurs all the way down his gullet."

"Oh, give him a break," Drummond said, trying not to laugh. "He'll tell you what you want to know, won't you kid?"

"I tell!" Allen squeaked. "Tell anythin! No spur!"

With seeming reluctance, Shannon none too gently pulled the spur out of Allen's mouth.

"Well, I guess I can be reasonable about it as long as he's being helpful. If he stops being helpful, though, the spurs go down the throat, both of them, points first. You got that, Junior? *Points first.*"

"Okay, okay," Allen said, feeling the inside of his mouth with shaking fingers. "I'm sick of this whole Morgan thing anyway. Whaddaya wanna know?"

Nervously, his eyes straying occasionally to the spur that Shannon was holding prominently in front of his face, Kenny Allen told his tale. It was much as Holloway had said—Allen had been enticed by the charms of Amy Morgan into joining the plot. He had hired gunmen to make the attacks on Morgan's railroad, including the thefts, the robberies, the firebombing, the dynamiting of the hillside the day before, and the rifle attack on the coach as it was on its way back to Railhead City that morning. He admitted shooting the workers at end of track the day that Shannon had arrived there, and also acknowledged that it was he who had opened fire on Shannon in the woods the night Shannon interrupted his meeting with Amy beside the river.

"I didn't kill Morgan, though," he insisted, gulping down the whiskey that Shannon had placed before him to keep him talking. "I didn't even know Morgan was dead until I got to town today. We'd already planned to shoot up the train this morning—that didn't have nothing to do with Morgan being snuffed last night. They can't hang me for that, can they?"

"Only one way to find out," Shannon said. He produced a set of handcuffs from under his coat and fastened them tightly around Allen's wrists. "Let's take a little trip down to the territorial capital tomorrow and talk to a federal judge about it, shall we?"

Shannon had again broken the weakest link, and once again had his case.

"Maxwell," he said, as he entered the hotel lobby pushing the still-dazed Allen ahead of him, "did you send that telegram?"

"Yessir, Already got a reply."

He handed Shannon the telegraph form. It read:

Marshals arriving Canyon City tomorrow's train. Deliver prisoners to them for transport back to capital. Well done.

"Good," Shannon said. "Now, come on, Junior. We're going down the hall to have a little chat with your friends."

"You mean Dalton and those two Morgan women?" Maxwell said. "They left."

"Left?" Shannon said blankly. *"They left?"*

"Yessir. Checked out while you were up at the Emerald Palace."

Dragging the unwilling Kenny Allen with him, Shannon dashed along the corridor where the rooms were located, flinging doors open as he went. Maxwell had spoken the truth. The rooms that had been occupied by Dalton, Velda Morgan, and Amy Morgan were empty. Both the people and their belongings had vanished. Fuming over the ill fortune that had forced him to deal with suspected murderers in a city that had no jail to lock them up in, Shannon hurried back to the lobby with Allen still in tow.

"I'm sorry, Marshal," Maxwell said. "I told them you

wanted them to wait here for you, but they just laughed at me and left."

"Any idea where they went?"

"They had their bags taken down to the railroad—I heard them tell the wagon man to hurry because they were leaving for the east right away."

"Come on, Junior," Shannon said. "We've got a train to catch."

The three private coaches of the late Isaac Morgan were sitting on the siding, still connected to the westward-facing work train that had brought them back from end of track the previous evening. A crew was preparing to uncouple the work train engine from the coaches, and they were backing up another locomotive from the eastern side of the yard, ready to attach it to the coaches for the journey back down the river and out of the mountains.

"Where's Dalton?" Shannon asked one of the crew.

"He's inside with the ladies," the man said. "Guess he's taken over for poor Mr. Morgan. A real shame about Mr. Morgan's heart attack, isn't it?"

"Yes, a real shame. When are you scheduled to pull out for the east?"

"Mr. Dalton said they wanted to be moving within thirty minutes. We're just coupling up the engine now."

"Don't bother. These three cars aren't going any-where."

"I have to hook it up, Marshal," the railroad man said, looking puzzled. "Mr. Dalton said so."

"Don't couple the engine to those cars," Shannon said emphatically.

"But I *have* to," the railroad man said. "Mr. Dalton's the acting president of the railroad, and he said to hurry."

Shannon undid one of Allen's handcuffs and locked it to the rail of the observation platform of Morgan's office car.

"Don't go away, Junior," he said. "I'll be right back."

He walked around to the side of the eastbound engine which was in position at the end of the private cars, waiting for the coupling to be completed.

"I'm telling you again," Shannon said to the crewman. "I don't want this engine attached to these cars."

The railroad man was becoming annoyed now.

"Look, Marshal, I work for the railroad, not for you, so I have to do what Mr. Dalton says."

Shannon drew his six-gun and very deliberately fired three shots into the steam lines connecting the boiler with the driving mechanism of the engine. The heavy .45 slugs easily penetrated the metal lines, and hot steam spurted from the holes, making a high-pitched whistling sound. Everyone in the yard turned to look, and the train crewman Shannon had been talking to stood there with his mouth hanging open, staring in disbelief at the escaping steam.

"Why did you do that, Marshal? Now we can't move the train."

"That's the general idea," Shannon replied, replacing the three expended shells in the cylinder of the six-gun and re-holstering it. "And you can tell your crew that if anybody tries to attach another locomotive to this train before I say so, I'll shoot holes in them too."

As the boiler lost pressure, the spurting steam slowed, and the whistling sound gradually died away.

The valet, Wimble, came out onto the platform of the office car.

"Mr. Dalton and Mrs. Morgan want to know what the noise is about," he said nervously.

"Tell them someone was shooting rats," Shannon said.

"They want to know about our departure time too," Wimble mumbled, looking around for dead rats.

"You can inform them that they'll be leaving Railhead City very soon," Shannon replied. "One way or another."

Pat Kelly came running up with several of his men.

"We heard the shots," he said. "What's going on?"

"I'm glad you're here, Pat. I could use some help. This town's got no jail, and I have to hold young Allen and some other people at the hotel until tomorrow when the deputy U.S. marshals I've sent for get here. I'll need your men to guard the prisoners until then. Can you do it?"

"Sure. Who else besides the kid are we going to be guarding?"

"You wouldn't believe me if I told you," Shannon replied. He undid the handcuff holding Kenny Allen to the observation platform and recuffed Allen's wrists together.

"Come on inside the coach with me, will you, Pat?" Shannon said. "And have your men hold this juvenile delinquent out here until I send for him. The folks in there have a big shock coming to them."

Chapter Fifteen
Judgment Day

Velda and Amy Morgan were seated in the leather chairs of the sitting compartment, while Dalton was relaxing comfortably behind Morgan's desk. Wimble was just in the act of serving them brandy, and the air when Shannon walked in was one of happy celebration.

All joy went out of the room, however, as Shannon entered.

"What the devil is this, Shannon?" Dalton demanded, jumping up from behind the desk.

"You're under arrest for murder, Dalton. You and these two female vultures here."

"Arrest? Murder?" Dalton said. "What are you talking about?" There was a quaver in his voice as he uttered the words which told Shannon that Dalton was in no doubt whatsoever as to what he was talking about.

"It's no use, Dalton. Holloway talked. You murdered Morgan, and you're going to hang for it."

"This is ridiculous," Velda Morgan said. "Russell wouldn't hurt a fly."

"Maybe not, but he shoved a hatpin into your husband's heart last night."

"Hatpin?" Velda Morgan said scornfully. "What hatpin?"

"This one," Shannon said, slipping the long pin out of his belt and holding it up.

Velda Morgan's face went dead white. She turned to Dalton with fear in her eyes.

"I thought you threw that away!" she cried.

"Shut your stupid mouth, Velda," Dalton said.

"Not only did he not throw it away," Shannon said to Velda Morgan, "he also planted it in your room at the hotel today. He was trying to make sure that if I figured out how Morgan was killed, I'd find the murder weapon in your room and charge you with the murder."

"You did that?" Velda said to Dalton, an incredulous look on her face. "You were going to let me take all the blame?"

"I said shut up!" Dalton snarled. "He hasn't got anything on us. Holloway's dead."

"Yes, he's dead," Shannon said. "It must have made you very happy when poor old Arthur stepped off that chair today. But before he did, he told me everything I needed to know."

"What good does that do you?" Dalton laughed. "Dead men can't testify."

"Live ones can," Shannon said with a wicked smile. He turned to Kelly, who had been listening to all of this dumbfounded. "Bring in our little surprise, will you, Pat?"

Kelly's men escorted the handcuffed Kenny Allen into the compartment. Dalton uttered a filthy oath. Velda Morgan gasped and turned her head away. Amy Morgan dropped her glass, staining her dress with brandy, but she was too busy looking pop-eyed at Kenny Allen to notice.

"You see, my friends," Shannon said, "I know all about your little plan. The three of you conspired to murder Isaac Morgan, and you're all going to swing for it. I have my star witness right here, and he's going to sing like a canary at your trial."

"What did you tell him, Kenny?" Dalton demanded.

"Everything he wanted to know," Allen said. "You doublecrossed me, Dalton. You told me we were just trying to stop the Denver & Sierra Northern from getting through the pass. You didn't tell me you were going to kill Morgan. I ain't swingin' for that."

"Why you little . . ." Dalton said, starting forward.

Shannon's Colt was in his hand.

"Hold it right there, Dalton. Let's keep this party polite. The game's up folks. I have the facts, I have the murder weapon, and I have my witness. Go ahead, young Allen, tell them what you told me."

"Don't say anything more, Kenny, please," Amy said, reaching out a hand entreatingly toward Allen.

"I'll say what I want," Allen retorted. "You tricked me, you little witch. Does your mother know you and Dalton were hitting the hay together all the time you were pretending to be in love with me?"

"It's a lie," Velda Morgan gasped.

"It's the truth," Shannon replied. "Dalton and your daughter have been having an affair for weeks. After

Isaac was dead, Dalton was going to marry you to get his hands on the railroad stock, and then he and Amy were going to kill you. But after Morgan changed his will and left everything to Amy . . ."

"He did *that*?" Velda Morgan croaked.

"Oh, yes. A couple of weeks ago. And that made you expendable, Mrs. Morgan. After that, Dalton didn't have to marry you to get the railroad, and so they didn't have to wait to kill you. You're lucky you're still alive."

"You said you loved me!" Velda Morgan shrieked at Dalton. "All those things you said to me when we were together—and all the time you were having an affair with Amy?"

"Of course he was," Amy sniffed. "You didn't think he could stomach *you* for very long, did you?"

Velda was out of her chair, facing Dalton with her hands clenched.

"Is it true, Russell?" she cried, spittle flying from her lips. *"Is it true?"*

Dalton's shoulders were sagging, and there was despair in his face. Shannon knew then that he had won.

"Yes, it's true, you silly cow," Dalton said viciously. "You didn't really think somebody like me would fall in love with the likes of you, did you? Why, it made me sick every time I touched you."

Velda Morgan let out a piercing scream of rage. Seizing a paper knife from Morgan's desk, she leaped at Dalton, trying to drive the knife into his throat. Dalton recoiled, then drew a hideout derringer from his sleeve and fired it into Velda. She fell backwards into the chair, moaning in pain and clutching at her breast.

Caught off guard by this unexpected development, Shannon raised his six-gun to shoot Dalton. Before he could pull the trigger, Amy had leaped in between them, blocking Shannon's line of fire. Screeching obscenities, she grappled with Shannon, seizing his gun arm and twisting it to one side, preventing him from firing in Dalton's direction.

Dalton discarded the derringer and drew his .44 revolver from inside his coat.

"Drop the six-gun, Shannon!" he shouted. "I'm not bluffing! I'll kill you and everyone else in this room if I have to!"

In despair that he had been caught so foolishly off guard, Shannon reluctantly let the Colt fall to the carpet.

"You can't get away," he said to Dalton. "You've got no place to run to. I've disabled the engine you were planning to use for your escape, and more U.S. marshals are on the way. It's over, Dalton. Over. You're going to hang. Ever seen anyone hang, Dalton? If you're lucky, the fall breaks your neck. If not, you dangle there, slowly choking to death. Just like Arthur Holloway."

Amy had released Shannon's arm and fallen back to where Dalton was standing.

"I don't want to hang!" she wailed. "Will we hang, Russell?"

"*You* may," Dalton laughed, "but *I* won't. I'll make sure of that."

He caught Amy around the waist and pulled her in front of him, shielding himself with her body. Amy screamed and then began to cry.

"Don't anybody move," Dalton commanded. "First

one that tries anything, I'll blow this little tramp's head off."

"So much for true love, I guess," Shannon said.

Still holding the squirming Amy in front of him, Dalton moved to the door of the compartment that led toward the front of the train.

"Good-bye, old chums," Dalton cackled. "I'll see you later—in Hades!"

He reached behind him and jerked open the compartment door, throwing the sobbing Amy to the floor as he did so. He leaped through the door, slamming it shut behind him.

Shannon scooped his Colt off the floor and fired through the door. He was hoping that the blind shots would hit Dalton as he ran down the corridor beyond, but there was no shout of pain, no sound of a falling body.

Amy was groveling on the carpet, shrieking unintelligibly. Shannon lifted the hysterical girl from the floor and shoved her roughly into one of the leather chairs. Then he bent over Velda Morgan.

"Is Mrs. Morgan all right?" Wimble asked in a trembling voice. He was still standing by the desk, holding the brandy bottle from which he had been pouring when Shannon first walked in.

"She's dead," Shannon said. "Looks like Dalton has another murder to answer for."

Amy Morgan was huddled in the chair, crying uncontrollably.

"He would have killed me," she sobbed. "I don't understand it. He said he was in love with me!"

"He told your mother the same thing," Shannon

reminded her, moving cautiously toward the door through which Dalton had vanished.

"But I love him!" she wailed.

"Personally," Shannon said, trying the handle of the door, "I don't think you know the meaning of the word."

"But I was going to marry him!"

"Cheer up. Maybe they'll let you share the same cell in the death house."

Taking a deep breath, he cocked the Colt and threw open the bullet-riddled door. There was no one in the corridor.

"He's gotten away, boyo!" Pat Kelly cried.

"He won't get far. I'll catch him."

He started through the door into the corridor, then grabbed at one of the railings along the wall as the car lurched violently.

Then the train started to move.

"He's gotten to the locomotive at the other end of the train," Shannon said.

"But what's he think he's doing?" Kelly said, puzzled. "That's the work train locomotive. It's headed west, up the canyon. There's nothing up there but end of track."

The train lurched again, then began to pick up speed.

"He's probably planning to run the train out of town and then jump off somewhere while we're trying to figure out what to do back here."

"But he'd be afoot in the wild," Kelly said. "What good would that do him?"

"If he gets away into the woods, we might never find him. He could circle back to town, get a horse, and head over the mountain toward the other railroad's camp."

He started up the swaying corridor.

"Stay here with these people, Pat," he called back. "Keep an eye on Junior and little Miss Muffet. I'm going to try to get up to the engine and catch Dalton before he jumps."

Shannon hurried up the corridor and through the door at the end, crossing the swaying platform into the dining car. The cook was there, looking as if he was about to faint.

"What's going on, Marshal?" cried the cook. "Mr. Dalton came running through here with a gun, and then the train started up."

"It's a long story. Get back to Morgan's office car and stay there. You'll have plenty of company."

The train was moving faster with each passing minute. The engine, normally encumbered with heavily loaded flatcars and other rolling stock, was pulling only the light passenger coaches, and it was gaining speed at an astonishing rate.

Pretty soon it will be moving too fast for Dalton to jump off. Too fast for the rest of us to jump off too.

Still with his six-gun at the ready, he went quickly through the sleeping car to the door at the end. Pushing through it, he found himself on the open platform just behind the locomotive's tender. The train was swaying so violently that Shannon had to hold tightly to the railing with his free hand to keep from being thrown off.

I wonder if he's jumped already. He'll break his neck if he dives over the side now. He must still be in the engine cab.

But Shannon's path to the engine was blocked by the sheer wall of the tender. Holstering the Colt, he stepped over the rattling coupling and took firm hold of the small iron ladder that ran up the back of the tender. Looking down, he could see the ties of the roadbed flashing away beneath his feet so quickly that they were nothing but a blur.

If you lose your grip on this ladder, you'll go under the wheels and they won't even find enough of you to bury.

He put the thought from his mind and began to climb the ladder. Almost immediately he found himself looking over the tender toward the locomotive. The level of wood in the tender was low, and across the top of the pile he could see Dalton standing at the controls in the open cab of the engine.

As Shannon started to climb over the edge of the tender, Dalton looked back. Seeing Shannon straddling the rear wall of the tender, he swung around and fired his revolver at Shannon. Desperate, Shannon launched himself forward into the half-empty tender, falling heavily on top of the chunks of wood.

Partly protected by the woodpile, Shannon raised his head again. The engine cab was scarcely fifteen feet ahead of him now, and he could plainly see Dalton leaning out the right-hand window, looking up the track.

"It's useless, Dalton! There isn't anything ahead of you. In another few minutes you'll run out of rails. Toss the gun overboard and stop the train while there's still time."

Dalton left the controls and crouched down, looking over the front wall of the tender at Shannon.

"Time for what, Shannon? Time to hang?"

"Time to bring this train to a halt before you kill yourself and a lot of innocent people." Shannon had the Colt out again, hoping to get a shot at Dalton when he raised his head again.

"Forget it, Marshal," Dalton shouted, throwing another shot at Shannon. The bullet struck the billets of wood just in front of Shannon's face. "If I can't get away, I'll take you and all the rest with me. If you come any closer, I'll drive this engine right into the river with everyone aboard—everyone. You and that shrew Velda and Allen and all the rest."

"What about Amy? You'd kill her too?"

"Why not? She got me into this. It was all her idea, Shannon—all of it. I'd like to see her at the bottom of the river. The world would be a better place without her."

The train was rocketing through the turns. Over the noise of the engine and the roar of the wind in his ears, Shannon could hear Dalton feeding more wood into the firebox.

"Slow down, Dalton. If you don't, this iron beast will go off the rails before you even get to end of track. Slow down, or I'll have to shoot you and stop the train myself."

"Shoot me then. I don't care anymore!"

He fired two more shots back into the tender, but the bullets went wild.

Shannon realized the situation was desperate. He couldn't go forward without exposing himself to Dalton's gun, but if he went back, there was nothing to stop Dalton from carrying out his threat to kill everyone on the train by running it off the rails. There was only one chance to save the people on board, and he had little time in which to try it.

Gathering himself for the effort, Shannon jumped up and swung back over the rear edge of the tender, again climbing down the swaying ladder. As the roadbed sped past beneath him, and with his heart in his mouth and his left hand holding the lower rung of the ladder with a grip of steel, he reached down toward the coupling connecting the sleeping car to the tender. Grasping the coupling pin, he heaved upward with all of his strength. If he could pull the pin, the cars would uncouple from the tender and roll harmlessly to a stop. But the pin would not budge. With the full weight of the moving train locking it in the coupling, it was beyond any one man's strength to move it. Again Shannon pulled with all of his might, gasping with the effort, but the pin was seemingly frozen in the coupling.

He had almost given up hope when suddenly the wheels of the tender encountered a small hump in the rails. Some track gang had not smoothed out the roadbed sufficiently to eliminate the bump, and as the tender's wheels struck the irregularity there was a fleeting moment when the tender was traveling a fraction slower than the sleeping car behind. The sleeping car moved forward infinitesimally toward the tender, loosening the coupling for a split second. Shannon was still heaving, straining every muscle, and the coupling pin came out, slipped out of his hand, and bounced away beneath the sleeping car.

Relieved of the weight of the cars behind it, the

engine leaped forward, and immediately the sleeping car began to fall away behind the tender. Now no longer being pulled by the engine, the three cars started to slow as they rolled up the slight grade. Dangling from the tender ladder, Shannon watched almost hypnotized as the gap between the tender and the front platform of the sleeping car gradually widened, leaving him stranded on the tender behind the speeding locomotive. If the detached coaches slowed soon enough, they might come to a halt before they reached the end of the track, and then the people in them would be safe. But would the cars stop in time?

Nothing I can do about that now, Shannon thought, starting back up the ladder. *First I have to get the locomotive stopped.*

He jumped over the rear wall of the tender and started forward on the piles of wood again. Dalton poked his head over the front of the tender and fired still another shot at Shannon, but the wild gyrations of the speeding locomotive caused him to miss once more.

Shannon slid to the side of the tender and looked out. Ahead, scarcely a mile away, loomed the log barrier that marked the end of the tracks. A minute to disaster, perhaps less. It was now or never.

He leaped to his feet and ran along the top of the woodpile toward the engine cab. Just as he reached the front of the tender, Dalton popped up again, aiming his six-gun at Shannon. Shannon fired, but the lurching of the tender spoiled his aim, and the slug struck Dalton in the left shoulder, spinning him around and throwing him back against the firebox. Even as he lay there, he raised his revolver and sent another bullet in Shannon's direction, forcing Shannon to duck back down behind the front wall of the tender.

"Stop the engine, Dalton! We're almost at end of track!"

"Not a chance, Shannon." Dalton was barely audible over the noises of the straining engine and the bucking tender. "You've ruined all my plans, but I'll have the last laugh. Come on, lawman, let's go meet the Devil together!"

The cowcatcher of the locomotive smashed into the log barrier at the end of the tracks, sending the logs flying into the air. The engine plowed through the debris and off the end of the rails, the spinning wheels digging deep into the gravel of the trackless portion of the roadbed. The engine shuddered as it roared through the gravel, ripping away ties and sending showers of stones up around it. The driving wheels, now buried in the roadbed and unable to turn, ceased their motion in a howl of tortured steel, as gears and pistons and driving rods shattered like glass. To Shannon, hanging on for dear life in the tender, it seemed as if the engine was screaming in pain.

Then the locomotive lurched to one side and began to tip over. The tender leaned after it, and Shannon saw that both locomotive and tender were going to roll off the edge of the hill. He had to get out of the tender before it went completely over. Knowing full well that at their present speed he had little chance of surviving, Shannon hauled himself over the high side of the leaning tender and jumped for his life.

The roadbed came up and hit him like a brick wall.

He bounced head over heels, rolled for a dozen yards along the rough gravel, and then lay still, astonished to find himself still alive. Shaking off the shock of the impact of his body with the ground, he looked up just in time to see the engine and tender go sliding over the edge of the gorge, amid the screeching of tortured metal and the splintering of the trees that clung to the slope. Ignoring the pain that seemed to lance through every bone and muscle in his body, Shannon scrambled up and staggered to the edge of the gorge, looking down at the drama.

The engine had separated from the disintegrating tender. The wreckage of the tender crashed to a stop amid the rocks on the hillside, but the engine, far heavier and with greater momentum, was still ploughing down the side of the canyon, shedding pieces of metal as it tumbled toward the river. To his horror, Shannon saw Dalton come flying out of the engine cab, his arms and legs flailing the air as if he was some sort of limp rag doll. His body bounced off a tree and then struck the rocks at the river's edge ahead of the plunging engine. Just before it reached the river, the locomotive slammed into a large rock outcropping, seemed to hesitate for one split second, then flipped end over end and came down right on top of the flat rock where Dalton's body lay spreadeagled. Shannon thought that in that last moment he heard Dalton scream, but amid the thunderous noises of the engine's passage down the slope, he couldn't be sure.

Then the engine's boiler exploded. The roar was earth-shaking, and the force of the explosion sent huge chunks of metal ripping through the trees and bouncing off the rocky wall of the gorge. Some of the jagged pieces of cast iron went splashing into the river, raising huge geysers in the tumbling water.

After that, there was only silence.

Chapter Sixteen
Aftermath

When Kelly and his men reached the scene of the wreck, they found Shannon sitting on a rock by the rim of the river gorge, looking down at the shattered engine at the water's edge.

"Are you all right, Marshal?" Kelly said, noting Shannon's torn coat and dirtied trousers.

"Bumps and bruises," Shannon said indifferently. "I've had worse from being thrown off a horse. Did you get the coaches stopped all right?"

"It was close, but luckily that last mile before the tracks run out is an upgrade. I put my men to work dogging down the brake wheels on the coaches, and we got them stopped just in time. How did you ever manage to get the cars uncoupled while the train was moving at that speed?"

"Desperation. And a little luck."

"A lot of luck for us." Kelly looked down into the gorge at the remnants of the tender and locomotive. "If you hadn't gotten those cars detached, we'd be down there with the rest of that pile of junk. Where's Dalton?"

"He's underneath the engine. Your railroad's going to need a new vice-president."

Helped by Kelly, Shannon made his way shakily back down the track to where the three coaches sat halted, scarcely a hundred yards from the end of the rails.

"Your men watching Junior and dear little Amy?" Shannon asked.

"Got Junior handcuffed to the desk, and Amy tied to the chair. That child knows some cuss words even my railroad crew never heard before."

"How do we get back to Canyon City?"

"I've sent one of my people hot-footing back down the track to get the other locomotive sent up here to haul us back to town. Shouldn't take too long—if they can plug the holes you put in the steam lines."

It was after dark before the headlamp of a locomotive could be seen winding its way up the track toward them. The coaches were coupled up, and they were soon on their way back down the rails to Canyon City.

When the engine had ground safely to a halt in the railroad yard, Shannon stepped stiffly down from the car and looked around him. A crowd was gathering as curious railroad workers and various citizens of Canyon City responded to the rumors about the wreck of the stolen train. Shannon made his way through the throng, followed by Pat Kelly's guards leading Kenny Allen and Amy Morgan. He took them to the hotel, where the faithful Maxwell was, as usual, behind the desk.

"Have you got a room in this hotel where I can safely lock up two prisoners for a few hours?" Shannon asked, indicating Kenny Allen and Amy. "Preferably one without any windows?"

"Got something better than that," Maxwell said. "There's a root cellar out back. It has a nice strong lock on the outside of the door to keep out thieves. Reckon that would hold them. Kinda dark and uncomfortable down there, but it serves them right for all the trouble they've caused in this hotel."

"Perfect," Shannon said. "Show the guards where it is, will you? Men, lock these two in the root cellar and stay by the door. Don't let them out until the marshals get here on the train tomorrow. I'll arrange some relief for you and some supper for them."

"Heck," Maxwell said with a mischievous grin, "you don't need to send them any supper. There's some old potatoes and dried up turnips down there in that cellar, left over from last winter."

"I guess that will do for the moment," Shannon said, "but I'll be back later to see if they want any dessert."

Chapter Seventeen
Going Home

Shannon entered the Emerald Palace saloon one final time to say good-bye to Tank Drummond.

"Thank you for all of your help," Shannon said to the saloon owner. "I'm glad our trails crossed again. Good luck with your place, here."

Drummond shook his head.

"It won't be here much longer," he said. "One of two things is going to happen. Either the Denver & Northern Sierra will make it through the mountains, in which case all of the people here will be moving west with the railroad, or else the company will go bust, and everyone will lose their jobs and drift off to find work someplace else. However it turns out, Railhead City will wither away until it's just a collection of empty, decaying shacks, inhabited only by the ghosts of the people who've died here."

"So you'll be moving on too."

"You bet," Drummond replied firmly. "You can't make any money selling whiskey to ghosts."

197

"Well, perhaps I'll see you in another saloon in another town. "Maybe the next Emerald Palace will be as grand as the old one back in Longhorn."

"Maybe," said Drummond with a wistful smile. "Or maybe those days are gone forever. Times change, Clay, and we all have to change with them. Even you."

Shannon stood on the station platform, waiting to board the eastbound train.

Pat Kelly stepped down from one of the coaches onto the platform.

"I've put your gear aboard," said Kelly. "Conductor says they're pulling out in about ten minutes."

"Thanks, Pat." Shannon was very tired and his muscles still ached from the fall from the doomed train two days before. A shrill whistle sounded at the other end of the yard, and Shannon could see a work train gathering speed as it started westbound up the canyon.

"I hear the railroad's laying track again," Shannon said.

"Yeah," Kelly replied. "The new owners got in last night. They're going to push on through the mountains, just like Morgan wanted. If they can beat the St. Louis, Salt Lake & Western through the pass, they'll all be rich men, and me and all the other poor slobs who'll lay the rails and drive the spikes for them will still be breaking our backs for a dollar a day at some other end of track."

Shannon chuckled.

"You're a railroad man, Pat. You wouldn't be happy doing anything else."

"I suppose so. If you work at something long enough, it gets in your blood, I guess."

"I know how that is," Shannon said, glancing down at the marshal's badge on his chest. "After a while, you just can't quit. Strange, isn't it?"

"I saw the other marshals putting Kenny Allen and Amy Morgan on the early train. Taking 'em back for trial, I suppose. What will happen to them? Will they hang?"

"It's possible, but I wouldn't bet on it. Kenny's father will hire a couple of dozen lawyers to defend him, and Amy will probably have half of the men on the jury proposing marriage to her right after they acquit her."

Kelly laughed.

"It would be funny if they both got off," he said, "and Kenny wound up marrying Amy after all."

"It might not be so funny for Kenny," Shannon replied, "especially if he inherits his father's railroad. Being rich and being married to Amy would be a hazardous combination. Kenny could have a short life expectancy. In fact, he might be better off just letting them hang him right now."

"I dunno," Kelly said wistfully. "I wouldn't mind being rich and married to somebody as good looking as Amy Morgan. It might not last long, but at least it wouldn't be boring."

The conductor came by.

"Two minutes, folks," he called. "Pulling out in two minutes."

Shannon shook hands with Pat Kelly.

"Thanks for everything, Pat. Without your help, I'd never have gotten through this alive."

"Ah, go on with you now," Kelly said with a grin. "You'd have managed just fine without me. You just keep that Colt of yours well-oiled and that badge nice and shiny, and you'll be all right. Maybe we'll meet again in some crummy railroad camp somewhere."

"Make it Denver or St. Louis. I've seen enough railroad camps for a while."

The conductor was shouting "All aboard!" With a last good-bye to Pat Kelly, Shannon climbed the steps of the waiting coach. The conductor swung up behind him, and with its bell ringing jubilantly the train began to move, headed back down the canyon, eastbound and away from Railhead City.

As they drew away, Shannon waved to Pat Kelly, then entered the coach and sat down next to the seat where his gear was piled. He settled onto the seat cushions and stretched his legs out, the tension draining from him as he relaxed for the first time in many days.

The conductor came along the aisle with a telegraph form in his hand.

"You're Marshal Shannon, ain'tcha?"

"When last seen," Shannon replied.

"Yeah, well, this came for you just before we left."

The conductor handed the telegram to Shannon. Shannon took the paper and read it.

Your son born last night. The baby and I are both well and he and I wait anxiously for your return. All my love. Charlotte

Shannon smiled, folded the telegram carefully, and slipped it into his pocket. He leaned back in his seat to watch the passing scenery, but soon drowsiness overtook him and he drifted off to sleep, at last a happy man.